"GOOD GRIEF, SAMANTHA, YOU HAVE A GUN!"

"Of course I have a gun, Tobin—and a license to carry it. I'm a private investigator, in case you've forgotten."

"Well, that tears it. You're out here alone in the middle of the night with a gun, waiting to catch a criminal. What do you expect to do if you actually see one?"

"Use my gun, if I have to," she answered angrily.

"And probably end up shooting your own foot."

"I happen to be a crack shot, and I have the trophies to prove it. Now, go home and let me do my job."

"I'm staying, damn it! I couldn't live with myself if I let something happen to you."

Samantha stared at him incredulously for a moment, trying to control her fury. "You know, Tobin, I hate this kind of macho stuff. Now, get going before I'm tempted to use *you* for target practice!"

CANDLELIGHT ECSTASY ROMANCES®

426 FANTASY LOVER, *Anne Silverlock*
427 PLAYING WITH FIRE, *Donna Kimel Vitek*
428 JUST A LOT MORE TO LOVE, *Lynn Patrick*
429 HOT ON HIS TRAIL, *Lori Copeland*
430 PRISONER OF PASSION, *Suzannah Davis*
431 LOVE MAKES THE DIFFERENCE, *Emily Elliott*
432 ROOM FOR TWO, *Joan Grove*
433 THE BITTER WITH THE SWEET, *Alison Tyler*
434 DARE TO LOVE AGAIN, *Rose Marie Ferris*
435 THE THRILL OF HIS KISS, *Marilyn Cunningham*
436 DAYS OF DESIRE, *Saranne Dawson*
437 ESCAPE TO PARADISE, *Jo Calloway*
438 A SECRET STIRRING, *Terri Herrington*
439 TEARS OF LOVE, *Anna Hudson*
440 AT HIS COMMAND, *Helen Conrad*
441 KNOCKOUT, *Joanne Bremer*

QUANTITY SALES

Most Dell Books are available at special quantity discounts when purchased in bulk by corporations, organizations, and special-interest groups. Custom imprinting or excerpting can also be done to fit special needs. For details write: Dell Publishing Co., Inc., 1 Dag Hammarskjold Plaza, New York, NY 10017, Attn.: Special Sales Dept. or phone: (212) 605-3319.

INDIVIDUAL SALES

Are there any Dell Books you want but cannot find in your local stores? If so, you can order them directly from us. You can get any Dell book in print. Simply include the book's title, author, and ISBN number, if you have it, along with a check or money order (no cash can be accepted) for the full retail price plus 75¢ per copy to cover shipping and handling. Mail to: Dell Readers Service, Dept. FM, P.O. Box 1000, Pine Brook, NJ 07058.

THE PASSIONATE SOLUTION

Jean Hager

A CANDLELIGHT ECSTASY ROMANCE®

Published by
Dell Publishing Co., Inc.
1 Dag Hammarskjold Plaza
New York, New York 10017

Copyright © 1986 by Jean Hager

All rights reserved. No part of this book may be reproduced or transmitted in any form or by any means, electronic or mechanical, including photocopying, recording or by any information storage and retrieval system, without the written permission of the Publisher, except where permitted by law.

Dell ® TM 681510, Dell Publishing Co., Inc.

Candlelight Ecstasy Romance®, 1,203,540, is a registered trademark of Dell Publishing Co., Inc., New York, New York.

ISBN: 0-440-16777-9

Printed in the United States of America

July 1986

10 9 8 7 6 5 4 3 2 1

WFH

To Our Readers:

We have been delighted with your enthusiastic response to Candlelight Ecstasy Romances®, and we thank you for the interest you have shown in this exciting series.

In the upcoming months we will continue to present the distinctive, sensuous love stories you have come to expect only from Ecstasy. We look forward to bringing you many more books from your favorite authors and also the very finest work from new authors of contemporary romantic fiction.

As always, we are striving to present the unique, absorbing love stories that you enjoy most—books that are more than ordinary romance. Your suggestions and comments are always welcome. Please write to us at the address below.

        Sincerely,

        The Editors
        Candlelight Romances
        1 Dag Hammarskjold Plaza
        New York, New York 10017

THE PASSIONATE SOLUTION

CHAPTER ONE

"You want me to buy a camera that looks like a pack of cigarettes?" Having just returned from lunch Samantha Preston sat on her battered metal desk, dangling her blue-jean-clad legs. She raised her green eyes from the clipping in her hand to confront those of Billy Bob Digby, her secretary. Since Billy Bob was a lanky six feet four, she had to raise them quite a distance. Her auburn brows were arched in an expression of disbelief.

Billy Bob thrust his hand into a pocket of his khaki trousers and pulled out a second ad clipped from a magazine. "This too," he said in his thick Texas drawl.

Samantha took the crumpled ad and read: *Amazing! You have to see it to believe it! Record conversations covertly with our Tricky Fountain-Pen Tape Recorder. It writes too! No private eye should be without one—or several! Only $19.95 while supply lasts.* Samantha handed both ads back to him. "Been reading *Startling Detective* again, Billy Bob?"

"Why do you always say that like it's a porn rag

or something? It's a good magazine. Last month's issue was devoted to mass murderers."

"Wonderful." Samantha slid off the desk and opened the office door. She pointed to the black letters on the frosted glass pane. "See that? What does it say?"

Billy Bob looked puzzled. "Sam Preston and Associates," he read. "Private Investigators." He shrugged. "So?"

Samantha stared into the empty hallway for a moment, thinking that she should have *Sam* changed to *Samantha*—as soon as she had twenty dollars to spare. She shut the door, went behind her desk, and sat down. "If I buy those trinkets, I can't pay the April rent. If I don't pay the April rent, the sign on that door will say Loo's Chinese Laundry or Fancy Dan's Tuxedo Rental Service."

Billy Bob eased his bony frame into his steno chair. "Aw, Samantha, they aren't trinkets. They're tools of the trade." He tapped his fingers idly over the typewriter keys, watching Samantha from the corner of his eye. "If I had that camera and recorder, it would be a breeze for me to get all the evidence we need in divorce cases, and free you for the important stuff."

Samantha wondered what important stuff Billy Bob had in mind. Since her Uncle Sam's death ten months previously the agency's business had dwindled alarmingly. Sam Preston had built up a solid reputation among Philadelphia's law firms; but since his death most of his clients had stopped using the firm for investigative work because they didn't trust a woman PI. Consequently Samantha's business consisted mostly of searching out evidence that could be used to obtain divorces and digging through old public records at the request of attorneys whose financial state was hardly better than her own. Lately it had been a struggle just to pay the rent and Billy Bob's salary.

At the moment Billy Bob looked so dejected, Samantha felt sorry for him. An avid reader of detective novels, her secretary imagined himself in the role of a hard-boiled private eye. But at twenty he lacked the maturity and experience to be an investigator. Maybe with time . . . "Billy Bob, why do you want to be a detective, anyway? You're the best secretary the agency's ever had. Can't you be satisfied with that for a while?"

He heaved a sigh. "I want to be where the action is."

Samantha suppressed a wry smile. She'd like to see a little action herself. Last night she'd gone through the agency's income-and-expense records for the past three months. It was painfully obvious that if she didn't bring in more clients soon, she'd have to close the doors. Aunt Ruby would love that! Sam's wife hadn't spoken to Samantha since the reading of Sam's will, which had left the agency to his niece.

Samantha had lived with Sam and Ruby from the time she was ten, when her parents were killed, until she was eighteen, when she went to work for her uncle full time. Sam, her father's only brother, had been a loving substitute parent, but Samantha had always known that Ruby didn't want her. Ruby had done her "duty" by Samantha "for Sam's sake," but it was done grudgingly.

When the will was read, Ruby's resentment came spilling out. "We've done more than enough for you already!" she'd shouted at Samantha. "Sam wasn't in his right mind when he made that will! If he had been, he'd have known you can't run the agency alone. If you had a grateful bone in your body, you'd sign it over to me now, while it's still worth something." But Sam had made Samantha promise not to let Ruby browbeat her into giving up the agency, so she walked out of the lawyer's office in the middle of Ruby's tirade and hadn't heard from her since. If she had to close down the agency, Ruby would undoubtedly break her silence long enough to say, "I told you so."

Samantha began shuffling through the papers on her desk while talking to Billy Bob. "Maybe when business picks up and I can afford an answering machine, you can get out of the office now and then. Do legwork." She lifted a file folder to look beneath it. "Didn't you say I had a couple of messages?"

"Next to the phone," Billy Bob said. "Samantha, do you really mean it? You'll give me a chance to do some investigating?"

Samantha nodded absently as she read the first message from a lawyer who hadn't paid her for the last job she'd done for him. She crumpled the note and tossed it into the wastebasket. She read the other message through a second time before she could believe what it said. "This is from Tobin Fitzgerald the Third! Why didn't you tell me?"

Billy Bob looked blank. "Who's he?"

"Only a member of the most prestigious law firm in Philadelphia. Fitzgerald, Fitzgerald and Fitzgerald. You've heard the name, surely."

"Sounds kinda familiar."

Samantha rolled her eyes. "Billy Bob, before Uncle Sam died, the Fitzgerald firm did a lot of business with the agency. We need them as clients. If I can land this assignment, the word will get around—and other good firms will give me a chance."

"Oh. Well, that Fitzgerald guy sounded like he'd already made up his mind to hire you."

Samantha felt a tingle of excitement at the base of her skull. Maybe her luck was about to change. "Exactly what did he say?"

"Just what I wrote there. He said he wanted the head of the agency to come to his office at three o'clock today to discuss an assignment. If it's not convenient, you're supposed to let his secretary know."

"Not convenient? Hah!" She waved a hand at her empty appointment calendar. "I think I can rearrange my schedule to squeeze in Mr. Fitzgerald." She looked at her watch. "Good Lord! It's already one-thirty. I can't go there in jeans! I have to go home and change." She grabbed her purse and headed for the door. "May I borrow your car?" Samantha's eight-year-old Chevrolet was in the garage for a major overhaul. She hadn't yet figured out where the money for the repair bill was coming from.

"Take it," Billy Bob said. "I'm not going anywhere till quitting time."

"Thanks. If that ambulance chaser Waylon Rutger calls again, tell him I'm in the Bahamas on a case and probably won't be back for a month."

"You wish."

"Yes, indeed!" Samantha grinned over her shoulder as she opened the door. "Oh, and if anybody else calls, you might just mention that I'm in a meeting at the Fitzgerald firm. A little PR never hurts. I've got a feeling, Billy Bob, that this is our lucky day. We may actually get to the Bahamas while we're still young enough to enjoy it."

"I'd settle for a Tricky Fountain-Pen Tape Recorder," Billy Bob grumbled as she shut the door behind her.

Samantha lived less than a mile from the agency in one of Philadelphia's neglected urban neighborhoods. That is, it had been neglected until recently when the city council designated it as an area where abandoned houses were available to urban homesteaders. Two years previously Samantha had submitted plans for the renovation of a shabby, but basically sound, two-story frame house. The plans were accepted, and she had moved in. The renovation was going slowly, since she was doing most of the work herself.

The neighborhood had taken on a new vigor during the past two years. Almost every house in Samantha's block was undergoing a face-lift, and she enjoyed the diversity of her neighbors.

Churchill, her aged bulldog, began barking

when Samantha fitted the key in the front door. Churchill had a withered back leg and hopped about on three limbs. Samantha wasn't sure he would be able to run as fast as a burglar, should the occasion ever arise, but his bark sounded fierce.

"It's okay, Churchill," she called as she opened the door. "It's only me."

The dog hobbled forward to greet her. She bent to rub him fondly behind the ears. Churchill had turned up on her doorstep about six months previously, evidently abandoned by his former owner. He wasn't the first dog she'd had since she moved into her house, and he probably wouldn't be the last. Samantha was a pushover for homeless animals. At present she also had three cats living with her.

Samantha hurried to her closet with Churchill at her heels. With a dissatisfied frown she scanned the closet's contents. "I want to look very yuppie," she told the dog as she examined a brown cotton dress.

Churchill cocked his head.

"No, too schoolmarmish. My mind must have been elsewhere when I bought that dress."

She rejected one after another of the garments —mostly jeans, slacks, shirts, and sweaters, her usual working attire—and a few dresses that showed their advanced age. Hanging at the back of the closet was the tailored, gray wool pinstripe suit she'd bought when she became head of the agency, because it made her look businesslike and older than her twenty-four years. It had been an impulse purchase, and afterward she realized she didn't really like the suit. But it might be appropriate for her meeting with Tobin Fitzgerald III. Actually, it was the only thing she owned that came close.

She put on the suit with a pristine white blouse that tied in a prim bow beneath her chin. Worn with plain gray pumps and a matching bag, the suit didn't look bad, Samantha thought as she surveyed herself in the dresser mirror.

She grabbed a tissue and blotted the perspiration on her forehead. It was an unusually warm day, more like June than April, and the butterflies in her stomach didn't help either. She removed the jacket and draped a towel over her shoulders while she applied makeup. Normally she wore nothing more than a dusting of powder and soft-colored lip gloss; but now she added a liquid foundation, rouge, eyeliner, and mascara. Then she loosed her fine auburn hair from its braid and pinned it into a chignon.

Definitely better, she decided, as she ran a critical gaze over her reflection. She looked twenty-seven at least, and the powder base had made the golden freckles on her nose disappear.

It was after two, and the drive to the Fitzgerald building was several miles through a congested section of the city. She grabbed her purse and jacket and rushed down the stairs. Churchill tried valiantly to keep up with her, while yelping his displeasure at a departure so soon after her arrival. In the living room she remembered that Billy Bob's car wasn't air-conditioned and grabbed a magazine to use as a fan as she ran out the door. "Hold the fort, Churchill."

She arrived, breathless and perspiring, at the offices of Fitzgerald, Fitzgerald and Fitzgerald with five minutes to spare. The reception room was roughly the size of a football field, with acres of plush mauve carpeting deep enough to lose a dachshund in. The couches and chairs were upholstered in a soft dove-gray fabric, and the creamy ivory walls displayed several modernistic watercolors. The place reeked of respectability and money.

As she crossed the reception room, she restored as best she could the tendrils of hair that had escaped during the drive and now straggled about her face. Her fine hair simply refused to stay put, which was why she usually wore it loose or in a single braid down her back.

The receptionist looked like Vincent Price's twin sister. Her sleek black hair was wound in an intricate French knot, not a wisp out of place. She wore a wine silk dress with white collar and cuffs that cost two hundred if it cost a penny. *I'll bet she gets three times what I pay Billy Bob*, Samantha thought, *just for sitting here and looking formidable.*

"May I help you, miss?" The receptionist had a British accent. What else?

"I'm from the Preston Agency. I have an appointment with Mr. Fitzgerald the third."

The receptionist opened a leather-bound appointment diary. It was the only thing on the highly polished desk. When she looked up, she said, "Mr. Fitzgerald was expecting the head of the agency."

Samantha ignored the disapproving set of the woman's thin lips and she tried to ignore the perspiration that was trickling down the valley between her breasts as she said stoutly, "I *am* the head of the agency. Samantha Preston."

The receptionist rose without missing a beat. "Would you take a chair, please? I'll inform Mr. Fitzgerald of your arrival." Her composure was back in place. Neither her expression nor her voice now gave any indication that she had an opinion about the head of the Preston Agency, one way or the other. The receptionist for Fitzgerald, Fitzgerald and Fitzgerald was probably not allowed to have opinions.

Samantha sat down and fished some tissues from her bag to blot the film of perspiration on her forehead and upper lip. She felt another wayward lock of hair brushing her neck and hastily tucked it back in place. The wool suit had been a mistake. She sat stiffly on the edge of the chair, closed her eyes, and tried to picture snow scenes.

"Miss Preston, Mr. Fitzgerald will see you now."

Samantha jumped and her eyes flew open. She stuffed the damp tissues back into her purse. "Thank you."

"This way, please."

Samantha followed the receptionist down a wide hall that seemed to stretch for at least a block. At the end of the hall the receptionist tapped on a large black door with gleaming brass hardware. In the center of the door there was a small brass plate bearing a discreetly lettered name: TOBIN GRANTHAM FITZGERALD III. The receptionist opened the door a crack, nodded at Samantha, and walked away.

A blond secretary sat behind an ebony desk in the outer office. Her blue eyes took Samantha's measure. She had, of course, been prepared by the receptionist, and it was clear she didn't see young, female detectives every day of the week. She made no effort to disguise her curiosity.

"Mr. Fitzgerald is waiting. You may go in now." Her tone was the same one she might have used to say, "His Majesty can give you five minutes."

Should she crawl in on her knees or merely curtsy? Samantha stifled a nervous giggle as she stepped into the inner office.

"Come in, Miss Preston." The deep voice issued from the burgundy leather couch in a corner of the large office. Tobin Grantham Fitzgerald III came to his feet as he spoke. His newspaper photographs didn't do him justice, Samantha realized. She judged him to be about thirty-five. He was tall and lean in a navy vested suit. His aristocratic features were framed by dark hair, streaked with a few silver strands and worn in a neat, conservative style. His eyes were brown and intelligent. "Please sit down." He indicated the gray leather armchair facing the couch.

"Thank you." She sat and curled her hands together in her lap to keep from tucking in the lock of hair that fell over one ear.

Tobin Fitzgerald resumed his seat on the couch and gazed at her in measuring silence for a moment. Samantha shifted nervously. His brown eyes never wavered in their meticulous perusal. What was he thinking?

Tobin forgot his annoyance with the unexpected turn the situation had taken long enough to admire Samantha Preston. Her face was classically oval, with high cheekbones under honey-toned skin. Her nose was delicate and uptilted, her mouth full and sensual. Beneath her auburn brows her eyes were dark green, thickly lashed, and direct. For an instant he toyed with the idea of stringing her along, just to keep her there where he could look at her. But years of self-discipline and integrity in business dealings prevailed.

"I'm afraid there's been a misunderstanding, Miss Preston. It's entirely my fault, of course."

He's a gentleman, even when he's giving me the brush-off, Samantha thought unhappily.

"I was not aware," Tobin continued, "that Mr. Preston had retired."

"My uncle didn't retire, he died. Ten months ago."

He had the grace to look uncomfortable. "I'm sorry. I had no idea." He paused as though to give her time to take the hint and excuse herself. She stayed where she was.

Tobin cleared his throat. "Sam Preston handled numerous assignments for us in the past with discretion and efficiency, so when I needed a private investigator I naturally thought of him."

"I worked with my uncle for five years," Samantha said. "I can handle the assignment, whatever it is." She had no intention of giving up without trying to change his mind.

His arm lay along the couch arm. For a moment he looked at his fingers as they drummed slowly against the fine leather. "I'm sure you're a capable person, Miss Preston, but this job"—his teeth flashed in a dazzling smile, evidently meant to soften the rejection. The man certainly was handsome—"It's not a job for a woman. I'm sure you understand."

Samantha had heard that excuse more times than she could count during the past ten months. "No, I don't. Mr. Fitzgerald, let me be frank. I'm good at what I do, but that doesn't seem to cut much ice with the city's big law firms. Since I took over the agency, we've lost most of them as clients for the sole reason that I'm a woman. I had hoped that you might be different."

He arched a dark brow. "Are you accusing me of sex discrimination, Miss Preston?"

"If the shoe fits, Mr. Fitzgerald . . ."

He didn't reply immediately. He studied her so intently that it was an effort for her to keep her gaze steady on his. She recognized the appraisal and was determined not to be affected by it.

Finally he said, "What I had in mind could be dangerous."

She managed a charming smile. "In my work there is always the potential for danger. It's something I deal with regularly."

He gave her a long, dry look. "I'd never forgive myself if I gave you this job, and something happened to you."

Samantha was unimpressed by this gallantry. It implied that she needed to be protected. She cocked her head to the side. "In that unlikely event why would you blame yourself? You aren't responsible for me."

His long, aristocratic fingers resumed tapping the arm of the couch. He was thoughtful for a moment, then said, "Perhaps we'll be able to use your firm for other jobs, later on."

Samantha was in danger of losing her hold on her temper. She gave a quick, unladylike laugh. "I see. Don't call me, I'll call you. Right?"

She has a temper to go with that red hair, he thought, studying her and trying not to laugh at the wispy curls that framed her face. *I'd like to pull the pins out and let the rest of it go free and tangle my fingers in that coppery mass.* Tobin jerked his thoughts back from such uncharacteristic frivolity.

He gave her a sympathetic smile that both attracted and infuriated her. "If you must put it that way." His smile changed, became almost dashing and somehow amused.

Samantha felt confused for a moment. She looked away from him. "I don't have time to call a spade anything but a spade, Mr. Fitzgerald." Before she said something worse, something unforgivable, she got quickly to her feet. "As for later —well, there is a strong possibility that I won't be in business then."

Samantha walked to the door, aware that his eyes were on her. She was disappointed, frustrated, and angry with him, but a part of her was intrigued by him too. She knew exactly what kind of man he was, what kind of life he led. But warring with her disdain for what she considered the injustice of his being born wealthy was a trace of respect. He could have instructed his secretary to give her the brush-off. Instead he'd faced her himself.

He was watching the fluid, leggy way she moved. *Quite a woman,* he decided. Still, he was surprised to hear himself say, "Let me think it over. I'll discuss it with the senior partner and get back to you."

She hesitated, then turned back to hand him a business card. "You can reach me at the agency or at home. Both addresses and phone numbers are there." She was sure she would never hear from him.

He strode toward a massive desk in the center of the room. "I'll ask my secretary to see you out."

"Never mind. I can find my own way. Good afternoon, Mr. Fitzgerald."

Tobin lowered himself slowly into the chair behind his desk. He stared at the closed door for a long time after Samantha Preston had gone. His mental image of private detectives was in shambles. What was the world coming to? Samantha Preston had looked young and vulnerable; ridiculously, his protective instincts had been aroused. For a crazy instant there he'd had a strange urge to wrap his arms around her.

He looked at her business card. SAMANTHA PRESTON, PRIVATE INVESTIGATOR. So the crusty, middle-aged detective he'd dealt with in the past had been dead for ten months. His secretary had slipped up. She should have noticed the newspaper obituary and brought it to his attention. He tossed Samantha's card on his desk and laced his fingers together behind his head. He expelled a long breath. Damn, he wished she hadn't told him how desperately she needed the job.

He returned some calls, then decided to quit for the day. For some reason he couldn't get Samantha Preston off his mind. He kept remembering those bewitching green eyes, that silky auburn hair, those golden freckles on her pert nose. What would happen to her if she had to close down the agency?

His reaction amazed him. He was usually very hardheaded in business matters. He made decisions based on the available evidence and didn't look back. He didn't need to confer with his father to know what this decision should be. He should call another agency. As she had pointed out, he wasn't responsible for what happened to Samantha Preston.

Still, he told himself, as he left the office shortly before five, he could show her the courtesy of telling her in person. Her address wasn't far out of his way.

He fingered her business card as he got into his Lincoln in the parking garage. He felt an anticipatory excitement suddenly. With a rumble of self-effacing laughter he started the motor. *Face it, old man, you're doing this for only one reason: You want to see her again.*

CHAPTER TWO

The block where Samantha Preston lived had probably been a pleasant residential street three decades earlier. Judging from the people Tobin saw, the neighborhood was now a mixture of middle-aged couples looking for bargain rents, older people on fixed incomes, and young families caught between the lower and middle classes. It struck him as an unsafe place for a young woman living alone. He had to remind himself that it was none of his business where Samantha Preston lived.

When he knocked on her front door, a dog barked inside. *At least she has some protection*, he thought.

Samantha opened the door and gasped. He looked totally out of place on her doorstep and even more attractive than he had in the hushed and formal offices of Fitzgerald, Fitzgerald and Fitzgerald. She had not expected to see him again, certainly not here.

Churchill barked frenziedly at the stranger. "Hush, Churchill!" Samantha commanded. "Go lie down." The dog whined his disagreement, but wobbled obediently away from the door. Tobin watched the crippled dog and thought, *Some protector.*

Her heart hammering, Samantha faced Tobin Fitzgerald again. Wanting her voice to be steady, she gave herself a moment before she said, "I wasn't expecting you, Mr. Fitzgerald." He had caught her in faded jeans and shirt, thongs on her feet, her hair braided, and without makeup. She was mortified and trying valiantly not to show it.

There seemed to be a quick flash of humor in his eyes. "I'm rather surprised to be here myself." He gave her a slow, thoughtful look. "May I come in?"

"Oh—yes, of course." She unhooked the screen and opened it.

He followed her into a large, high-ceilinged room. The walls had been painted chalk-white. The recently refinished hardwood floor glowed, and the unstained wood shutters at the long windows were folded back to admit the late-afternoon light. The living room was furnished with odd pieces of furniture, perhaps picked up at garage sales. Scattered around the room were numerous pots and baskets of greenery and flowering plants making it bright and cheerful. Samantha had done wonders, Tobin decided, on an extremely limited budget.

Churchill, who was prone but alert beside a cane rocker, watched Tobin cross the room.

"Please sit down." Samantha indicated a large armchair upholstered in a nubby spring-green fabric. She stood uncertainly in the center of the room for an instant, then said, "I was about to have a cup of herbal tea. Would you like one?"

Tobin leaned back in the chair. "Yes, thanks."

She left the room. The bulldog kept an intent watch on Tobin, who returned the perusal uneasily as he shifted in the chair. The dog growled low in his throat. "Vicious little bugger," Tobin muttered.

A white long-haired cat appeared from an adjoining room and wound itself around Tobin's legs. Grimacing, he lifted the cat, set it away from him, and picked white hairs off his navy trousers. The cat gave a disdainful flip of its tail and began to wash its paws. A few moments later Samantha returned with a tea tray which she placed on a low oak table near Tobin's chair. "I thought I put you out, Delilah," she said to the cat as she scooped it into her arms. She banished the cat to the porch, then returned to pour the tea.

"You like animals," Tobin observed.

She smiled. "Too much, I sometimes think. I have two other cats besides Delilah. I couldn't begin to tell you how many other animals I've found homes for since I moved in here. Most of them were cats and dogs, but I've had a gerbil and even a monkey for a short period of time. I'm a sucker for abandoned creatures who turn up on my doorstep." She handed him a cup of the steaming tea.

His fingers closed over hers as he accepted the cup with a trace of a smile. "Lucky for me."

Samantha refused to pull her hand free. They remained as though frozen for a split second, leaning toward each other, their fingers overlapping on the handle of the cup. She was surprised at the lightning response of her body to his touch, but she regarded him steadily. "You can hardly be described as abandoned, Mr. Fitzgerald."

"Tobin," he said softly as he reluctantly released her fingers to steady the cup with his free hand. He sampled the tea; it tasted of apples and cinnamon.

Though he was no longer touching her, her blood was still heated. She sat in the rocker and lifted her teacup. She felt his eyes on her and a warm flush spread up her throat. "I don't always go around looking like this," she apologized, "in old grungies with no makeup on. I've been cleaning house."

"Don't apologize, Samantha. It's a rare woman who's beautiful in her natural state." His dark eyes seemed to glitter for a moment, and Samantha felt her color deepening at the image evoked by his words. Somehow she knew he was imagining her in a *totally* natural state.

She gave a low, sultry chuckle that skimmed along his skin. She wrinkled her nose. "You think freckles are beautiful?"

"On you, yes." He smiled and lifted his cup in a silent toast. Was Tobin Fitzgerald III actually flirting with her? Amazing. He seemed so different from the man she had met earlier that afternoon—still consummately self-assured, but less superior and more relaxed. Now he was just a man letting a woman know that he found her attractive. Samantha felt the shock of that attraction in every pore.

Her breathing quickened, in spite of her efforts

to control it. In her living room his voice sounded lower and huskier and his intense gaze made her think of danger. She could actually feel her body respond to him, but she forced her thoughts along more acceptable paths.

"You know, Mr. Fitzgerald—"

"It's Tobin, Samantha," he insisted.

She shrugged. "You didn't have to come in person to tell me I'm not getting the assignment."

"That isn't why I came." He heard himself with a degree of shock. He had left the office with exactly that intention.

Samantha leaned over to set her cup in its saucer. "Oh? Why, then?" Her green eyes darkened, as though she were issuing a challenge.

He set his cup down beside hers on the tray, without taking his eyes off her. He had known many beautiful women—but he'd certainly never known a woman like Samantha Preston before. With the possible exception of his grandmother, Eleanor. In fact, it was actually his grandmother who wanted to hire a detective. Tobin had only taken on the chore to prevent her hiring somebody unscrupulous who might take advantage of a wealthy, elderly widow. Watching Samantha, Tobin saw that she, like Eleanor, had a strong mind of her own. They would probably get on well together.

What was he getting himself into?

"My grandmother, Eleanor, lives alone—except for the servants—on an estate outside of town. She's eighty-two and we've been trying for some time to get her to move into a smaller place nearer my parents or a retirement home. Unfortunately, she's as stubborn as they come and refuses to budge. She accuses us of trying to evict her from her home."

Samantha was listening absorbedly, wondering what this had to do with the assignment. She smiled at Tobin's description of his grandmother. "She would probably feel lost in new surroundings."

Tobin eyed her musingly. "So she says." He was right about Samantha. Without even meeting Eleanor she understood how she felt. "Anyway, several years ago she turned part of the estate into a nature preserve. Recently, somebody has been shooting the birds in the preserve. Some of them are rare specimens of endangered species, and naturally Grandmother is upset."

Samantha frowned. "No wonder. Who could be so cruel?" Her love for animals was in the deeply felt words.

Tobin felt reassured. Perhaps Samantha was the right person for the job after all. He didn't think he was offering it to her solely because he found her attractive. "She has no idea who's doing it—or why. I promised her I'd find an investigator for her. If you're interested in tracking down a bird killer"—he gave her a lopsided grin—"I'll take you out to meet Grandmother. You'll have to pass muster with her before you're hired."

Tracking down bird killers wasn't exactly big time, Samantha reflected, but at the moment her only requirement was that it be a paying job. If

30

Eleanor Fitzgerald approved of her, she'd have no problem collecting her fee on this one. "When?"

He laughed. "You don't even want to think it over?"

He seemed almost carefree when he laughed, and something in his eyes made a tremor skip up her spine. Heat flashed through her, as it had when he'd touched her. The flicker in his eyes was desire, she realized abruptly. Beneath his breeding and sophisticated veneer was a man she would need to be wary of, she concluded. Extremely wary. What she must do was to keep reminding herself who he was—a wealthy, class-conscious member of the Philadelphia gentry—and who she was. And of the chasm that yawned between them.

"I need the job," she said simply.

"Good enough. I'll pick you up here at nine tomorrow morning."

"Fine." She looked at him expectantly.

It was a moment before he realized they had concluded their business and he had no further excuse for staying. With an odd reluctance he got to his feet. The thought of leaving his present surroundings and returning to his hushed, immaculate, elegant house was an unwelcome one. He shook off the feeling and said good-bye.

Samantha watched his sleek black Lincoln until it rounded the corner at the end of the block and passed from sight. The prospect of seeing him again the next morning filled her with a mixture of anticipation and caution. She couldn't remember when she'd been so aware of a man on a deep, sexual level. Of course, he had invited that reaction with the way he'd looked at her, but it was partly her own fault for lowering her guard. She had enjoyed talking with him. Since her uncle's death she had missed conversing with a mature, intelligent man.

That was no excuse for the way she'd let him get to her, she told herself. He'd made her forget the vast distance that separated them . . . and he'd enjoyed it. Indeed, why shouldn't he? She was nothing to him, a toy that he found briefly amusing. She must remember that tomorrow morning. At the moment, though, she didn't want to dwell on it.

Restlessly, she wandered to the kitchen, where her gaze fell on the leash hanging on a hook near the back door. Taking it down she called, "Let's go for a walk, Churchill."

Tobin arrived at nine o'clock sharp, wearing tweed trousers with an open-necked shirt and comfortably worn western boots. Although the clothing had obviously been quite expensive when new, it didn't fit the proper, staid attorney who, Samantha had convinced herself during a restless night, was the real Tobin Fitzgerald. Anticipating tramping through Eleanor Fitzgerald's nature preserve, she was dressed in jeans, a long-sleeved cotton shirt, and boots; but somehow she had expected him to show up in a three-piece suit.

He smiled slowly. "Ready?" he inquired as she hesitated inside her front door.

She swallowed and threw a sweater over her shoulders. "Sure thing."

The white interior of the Lincoln smelled of fine leather and the faint musky odor of masculine cologne. Giving Tobin a long, silent look as he started the engine, Samantha drew sunglasses out of her shoulder bag and slipped them on.

The gesture seemed to amuse him. The sun had been behind a haze of clouds all morning. "You don't really need those," he said.

Samantha tossed her braid behind her shoulder, trying to disguise the annoyance she felt at the ease with which he saw through her defenses. "I'll be the judge of that."

"Okay," he returned amiably, amused at the temper that edged her words. *You feel the electricity between us, Samantha,* he thought, *the same as I do.* Last night he'd almost convinced himself he'd imagined it. But the moment she had opened her door and looked at him with those deep-green eyes, the sparks shot through him again.

She took advantage of the shield provided by the sunglasses to examine his profile. No, her memory hadn't exaggerated his striking good looks, she thought with an inward sigh.

Tobin was aware of her scrutiny and wished he knew what she was thinking. For some minutes they rode without further conversation. It was Tobin who finally broke the silence. They were passing through one of Philadelphia's most exclusive residential areas when he slowed the car. "This is where I live." For a reason that was not altogether clear to him, he had wanted to show her his house and had driven out of the way to do so.

Samantha stared as a Gothic mansion glided slowly past. The house was a soft pink with a steep roof, numerous angled eaves, and gray gingerbread trim—what the society page breezily called "a villa." It was surrounded by a variety of budding trees and a large, rolling green lawn. More than ever she was thankful for the sunglasses, which hid her wide-eyed stare. She knew he was wealthy, but the grand old mansion served to underscore the wide gulf that separated their two worlds.

"It's very nice." She laughed nervously. What an understatement. They were past the house now, and she settled back against the seat. "It seems awfully large for a bachelor." Tobin's name was frequently mentioned in the society sections of Philadelphia papers, and Samantha knew he'd been a widower for several years.

"My son is usually home on weekends."

Samantha's interest was piqued, in spite of herself. "I didn't know you had a son."

He made a sound that was not quite a laugh. "Sometimes I wonder myself if there wasn't a mixup in the hospital nursery and Grant is really somebody else's son." He caught Samantha's frowning concern and added hastily, "I'm only joking. It's just that, most of the time, we don't communicate very well."

Samantha's expression softened in sympathy. "How old is Grant?"

"Twelve." There was a tension in him when he

spoke of his son that made her want to reassure him.

"And he's Tobin Grantham Fitzgerald the Fourth."

Tobin's mouth twisted wryly. "Naturally. Fitzgeralds don't break with tradition easily, but Grant might be the exception. He says he's going to be a country-western singer." He said it in the uncomprehending way another man might say that his son wanted to be a female impersonator. To be an entertainer was evidently an unacceptable ambition for a Fitzgerald.

Samantha suppressed a smile. "But you think he should be a lawyer."

"It's an honorable profession."

"It isn't dishonorable to be a singer."

"Something tells me," he said with an ironic edge to his voice, "that you and Grant would hit it off."

"Your son and I have something in common," she agreed easily. "I happen to be a country-western fan myself."

"Perhaps you could explain its charm to me sometime."

"Perhaps," she murmured.

"You could do it over lunch. I thought we could go back to my house, after we talk to Grandmother."

She didn't even try to conceal her surprise. "For lunch? I wouldn't dream of putting you to so much trouble."

He shrugged. "No trouble. I've told my houseman to expect us."

She swiped a wayward wisp of hair off her forehead. Oddly, his offhand manner irritated her. Naturally he had servants. He'd grown up with servants to cater to his every whim. But why should that matter to her? "I don't think so," she said flatly. "I don't feel at home in this neighborhood." It seemed a good time to remind him of the difference in their backgrounds. "Besides, I hate caviar," she added with a touch of sarcasm.

"No caviar, then," he promised with a grin, "and I'll serve you only domestic champagne." He laughed at her sidelong glance. "You're a snob, Samantha."

"That's ridiculous," she retorted. "*I* wasn't born with a silver spoon in my mouth."

"There, you see." He caught the wisp of hair that had, once more, fallen across her forehead and twisted it around his finger. "Reverse snobbery if I ever heard it."

She pulled away. "Just the same, I don't care to have lunch at your house. I need to get to my office."

He lifted a brow. "Where your phone is ringing off the hook?" It was unkind of him to tease her about the paucity of the agency's business, but she had asked for it.

"I do have a few other clients besides you."

He pondered that in silence. They had left behind the congestion of the city and had entered Bucks County, where historic estates and sites abounded. Miraculously much of the area's natural beauty had survived major development.

"All right," Tobin said at length, "we won't have lunch at my house."

Samantha glanced over at him dryly. "Correct."

She turned to look out the side window at the river, and Tobin placed a firm hand on her arm. "Not this time."

Samantha gave the hand on her arm a long look before she raised her eyes to his. He smiled.

"There will be another time, Samantha." Reaching up he drew off her sunglasses and let them dangle between his thumb and index finger. "You know that as well as I do."

"Mr. Fitzgerald—"

"Tobin," he corrected, holding the sunglasses away from her when she reached for them. "Let me hear you say it."

Samantha stiffened. She ran her suddenly damp palms down her thighs. No man should be so sure of himself, damn it. "Tobin," she said coolly.

"Good." He handed her the sunglasses, "we're making progress."

"That's what you think," she muttered as she slipped the sunglasses back on. "And I'd feel a lot safer," she added, "if you'd keep your eyes on the road."

His gaze lingered on her mouth before he returned his full attention to driving. Within moments his relaxed silence unnerved Samantha as much as his flirtatious bantering had. "How much farther is it?"

The Delaware River formed the eastern boundary of Eleanor's estate, the entrance to which was immediately ahead. "We've arrived," Tobin said as he turned the Lincoln between two massive stone pillars. A long drive meandered through green lawn and finally led to a rambling stone house complete with ivy-covered walls and numerous leaded glass windows. The epitomy of the English manor house, Samantha thought as Tobin stopped the car on the circular drive in front.

An elderly man in a dark suit—the butler, probably—came to the door. His wrinkled face lit up when he saw Tobin. "Ah, Mr. Tobin, she's expecting you."

"How are you, Wilkins?"

"Can't complain, sir."

The interior of the house appeared to be a series of dark-wood-paneled rooms containing antique furniture. After seeing the house and the butler Samantha expected Eleanor Fitzgerald to be an elegant old lady in a black dress, her white hair arranged in an old-fashioned style.

She wasn't prepared for the tiny, spry black-eyed woman in knee-length trousers, knee socks, and sturdy walking shoes who came toward them as Wilkins ushered them into a book-lined study.

"I'd almost given you up, Tobin," she greeted her grandson. The short white curls all over her head bobbed as she walked.

Tobin chuckled and bent to kiss her lined cheek. "I said I'd be here this morning, Grandmother. Have I ever broken a promise to you?"

Eleanor reached up to pat his cheek fondly. Her black eyes twinkled. "I must admit, you haven't. But what took you so long?"

"We don't all get up at the crack of dawn," said Tobin.

"Well, you should," stated Eleanor. "The bird songs are the most beautiful then." Her sharp gaze came to rest on Samantha. "Who have you brought with you, Tobin?"

Tobin drew Samantha forward. "Samantha, this is my grandmother, Eleanor Fitzgerald. Grandmother, this is Samantha Preston, a private investigator."

This information clearly delighted Eleanor. She had the light, trilling laugh of a young woman. "You're a detective, my dear? How marvelously exciting."

"Not really, Mrs. Fitzgerald," Samantha told her. "It's actually pretty boring most of the time."

Eleanor's gaze raked Samantha's jeans and boots. "Good, you had the sense to wear something appropriate for a trek through the wild. We'll go straight to the preserve. You can wait here if you wish, Tobin."

"I'll tag along, Grandmother."

Eleanor gave him a surprised look, but shrugged and led the way from the study without comment. Tobin leaned over to speak low in Samantha's ear. "Congratulations. I think you're hired."

CHAPTER THREE

Samantha nearly ran to keep up with Eleanor Fitzgerald. Tobin ambled along behind the two women, occasionally smiling to himself as though he found the whole thing pretty silly. Samantha was too busy keeping up with Eleanor and listening to her talk about the birds in the preserve to be unnerved by anything Tobin did.

They tramped along narrow paths through close-growing trees. "My passion at the moment," Eleanor was saying, "is our whooping cranes. We have two pairs and we're hoping to get a flock started. Did you know, Samantha, that not many years ago there were only fifteen whooping cranes known to be living?"

"No, I didn't," Samantha replied, stepping carefully over a tangle of vines in the path.

"It's true," Eleanor said, shaking her head. "We were that close to losing them completely. Why, to lose the whooping cranes would be dreadful loss in terms of aesthetics alone. Fortunately, the situation has improved somewhat. Today there are nearly a hundred and fifty in existence, all descendants of those fifteen birds."

"They must not have large families," Samantha commented.

"The females usually hatch two chicks a year, but rarely do both survive. Trying to breed them in zoos hasn't been successful. The only hope for the whoopers is wildlife preserves such as this one. Oh, here we are. My caretakers should be around somewhere." They had reached a long, low, barn-like building. Eleanor halted and said in a low voice, "Nobody need know why you're really here. I have perfect faith in my caretakers, but the fewer people who know, the better."

A man who appeared to be in his seventies came out of the barn. "Hi, Ben," Tobin called.

The old man turned and came toward them. "You're the last person I expected to see out here, Mr. Tobin."

"I decided to find out what I've been missing," Tobin said amiably.

"Tobin has never been much of an outdoorsman," Eleanor explained to Samantha with a calculating glance at her grandson. "This is Ben, my dear. He's been with me for forty years. Ben, this is Samantha Preston, Tobin's friend."

"How do you do, ma'am?"

"I want to show her the cranes. Are they inside?"

"Yes'm. We've been feeding them inside and keeping them penned since the shooting started. Mike and Howard are feeding them now."

"Good. Come along, Samantha—Tobin." They parted from the old caretaker and Eleanor confided, "Ben's arthritis makes it impossible for him to do much work now, but he won't admit it. I told him recently he simply must take his pension and retire. He's been angry with me ever since."

Inside, two young men, one blond and one with dark-brown hair, were placing two whooping cranes in a large pen with two others at the far end of the building. Eleanor introduced them to Tobin and Samantha. Mike was the blond, Howard the dark-haired one. They were college students, they told Samantha, and only worked part time. They seemed to enjoy their work and handled the cranes as carefully as they might have fine crystal. "These are our pride and joy," Mike explained to Samantha. "We're hoping they're going to hatch some chicks."

"Mrs. Fitzgerald told me," Samantha said.

Eleanor talked to the cranes and quizzed the young men about their work. "We try to do things before Ben gets around to it, like you told us, Mrs. Fitzgerald," Howard said, "but it isn't easy. He resents any suggestion that he can't do the work he used to do."

"I know how Ben is," Eleanor said. "You'll just have to ignore him. He's retiring in June."

Samantha listened to the conversation and watched the cranes, fascinated. Tobin lounged against a wall, obviously bored.

Tobin watched Samantha and Eleanor engrossed in conversation with the two young caretakers about the wildlife on the preserve, and silently congratulated himself. As he'd suspected, Samantha and Eleanor were getting along famously. *Two of a kind*, he thought wryly.

He was glad when, a while later, Eleanor decided it was time to go back to the house. Once there, Eleanor invited them to stay for lunch. When Samantha said she needed to get back to her office, Eleanor insisted that they at least stay long enough for tea.

"Now, Samantha," Eleanor said, when they were seated in the study with hot tea and cookies, "if you're free next weekend, I'd like you to stay here at the estate. You see, all the shootings have occurred on Saturday or Sunday night."

"You mean I'm hired?"

Eleanor laughed. "My goodness, yes, I thought that was understood."

Samantha glanced at Tobin, who was watching her with a twinkle in his eyes. "I wanted to be sure. How many birds have been killed?"

"Six. One at a time. The shootings have been spread out over about six weeks." Eleanor shook her head sadly. "I can't imagine why anybody would want to kill poor, innocent birds. It simply doesn't make sense."

"It doesn't seem to," Samantha agreed.

"When did you tell Ben you were pensioning him off?" Tobin asked.

Eleanor looked at him sharply. "Why, a few weeks ago."

"Six weeks?"

"Possibly." Eleanor frowned. "I see what you're thinking, but, no, Tobin. Ben might be angry with me, but I can't believe he'd be so spiteful as to take it out on the birds."

Samantha met Tobin's look across the tea table.

She had been wondering about Ben herself. After a moment's pause he said, "Just a thought." But Samantha could tell he wasn't convinced of Ben's innocence; nor was she. She made a mental note to keep an eye on the caretaker during the weekend.

Before leaving, Samantha came to an agreement with Eleanor concerning her fee, and Eleanor gave her an advance. It was enough to pay the repair bill on her car, which she would need to drive to the estate on Saturday. There would even be money left over to pay the month's office rent.

Back in the car with Tobin, Samantha felt her self-consciousness returning. The sun had burned the haze away and now shone brightly. She donned her sunglasses, which elicited a knowing grin from Tobin.

"I like your grandmother," Samantha told him, for something to say.

"She liked you too. In fact, come to think of it, you're the first woman I've introduced her to since my wife died that she's approved of."

Samantha's hands tightened on the edge of her seat. She could easily picture the women Tobin had introduced to his grandmother—all of them beautiful, wealthy, refined. She thought it was cruel of him to refer to her as though she were in the same class with them.

"It's hardly the same thing," she finally said.

Tobin darted a sideways look at her face. "Why?"

She tried, and failed, to discern a teasing inflection in his tone. His voice was deep and apparently serious. She refrained from pointing out the most obvious differences between herself and the other women he had taken to Eleanor's estate, and settled for "The others were there with you."

"So were you," he reminded her easily.

"I was there on business."

"Ah. A fine distinction."

"No, a huge one."

He might have chuckled, but she couldn't be sure. He turned on the radio, found some symphony music, and leaned back against his seat to steer the car with one hand lightly touching the bottom of the wheel.

Samantha relaxed her fingers on her seat. "It was nice of you to drive me to your grandmother's. I could tell you weren't exactly thrilled with the trek through the preserve."

"I enjoyed it more than I'd anticipated." His face took on a thoughtful expression. "Did you?"

Samantha smiled. "It's part of the job."

Idly Tobin placed his free hand on the leather seat, touching hers. "That doesn't answer my question, Samantha."

She looked at his hand and lifted a brow. "I found it interesting."

"The whooping cranes or Mike and Howard?" he asked softly as he ran a fingertip over her knuckles.

Samantha vowed not to move her hand and give him the satisfaction of knowing how deeply his touch affected her. Instead she regarded him steadily. "Mike and Howard are children."

With a trace of a smile he shrugged. "They're only a few years younger than you."

"How old do you think I am?"

"Twenty-four." At her surprised look his brown eyes challenged her. "I checked."

She felt a warmth spreading through her body. She had to make him stop touching her. As carelessly as she could, she lifted her hand and rested it on her denim-covered knee.

"Don't you want to know how old I am?" he inquired.

She feigned an interest in the passing scenery. "Not particularly."

Unfazed, he went on, "I'm thirty-five. Is that too old?"

Even though her brain told her to ignore the question, Samantha couldn't resist trying to puncture his colossal self-confidence. "Depends."

"On what?"

"If you're thinking of trying out for the Olympic track team, I'd say it's too old."

He laughed. Lifting her hand from her knee he curled his fingers around it. *Small and soft and competent*, he thought. "You know what I mean, Samantha. Am I too old for you?"

She sucked in her breath. His hand was firm and warm and large enough to envelop hers completely. "Since the problem isn't likely to arise, the question isn't relevant."

"You sound very sure of that."

She made a low, ironic sound. "I am." She started to remove her hand, but his fingers tightened around it.

"Are you often wrong?" he murmured. His gaze

skimmed her controlled expression before returning to the road.

Common sense told her to shut up; the more she said, the more outrageous he became. But he had provoked her, and she couldn't keep quiet. "Not about this, I'm not," she said coolly. His only response was another chuckle. She said in an even colder tone, "I'd like my hand back."

The sunlight glittered off the sprinkling of silver hairs at his temple as he turned his head to give her a dashing grin. "Not just yet." Lifting her hand he pressed his lips deep in the center of her palm. Samantha felt the kiss race hotly through every vein in her body. "What was that you were saying about the problem not arising?" he challenged against her flesh.

Samantha's breath caught in her throat. She wasn't even aware that they were nearing her street; she wasn't aware of anything but his warm breath against her palm. Feeling her resistance melting away she summoned all her willpower. When his hold loosened, she jerked her hand away. "Don't you ever watch where you're going? You're the most dangerous driver I've ever had the misfortune to ride with."

"I can be even more dangerous," he said as he stopped the car in front of her house, "when I'm hungry."

Stunned by his audacity Samantha glared at him. "Are you suggesting that I feed you?"

"Yep."

"I don't have time. I'm going to grab a sandwich and go on to the office."

"A sandwich will do," he said easily, and climbed out of the car.

Samantha scrambled out of the passenger side and ran after him up her front steps. "Can't you take a hint, Tobin Fitzgerald?"

He thrust his hands into the pockets of his tweed trousers and gazed down at her. "It's your fault I'm not enjoying a delicious meal in my own house right now. You owe me lunch, Samantha."

He obviously had no intention of going away. Muttering, she turned her back on him and unlocked the door. She strode through the house to the kitchen without looking back to see if Tobin was following her. With angry movements she spread tuna fish salad between slices of whole wheat bread, made iced tea, and set the meal on the table.

Tobin sat down across from her. "Where's your watchdog?"

"I put Churchill and the cats in the backyard before I left this morning."

Tobin was relieved to hear it. He didn't trust that bulldog. And he didn't relish the prospect of spending a half hour picking cat hairs off his clothes. He tried one or two conversational gambits as they ate, but Samantha refused to cooperate. They finished the meal in silence.

When Samantha got up and carried the dishes to the sink, Tobin asked, "Do you want me to drive you to work?"

"It's not far," she said without looking around. "I'll walk."

"All right," he said reluctantly. "Well, I guess I'd

better go home and change. If I turned up at the office like this, the shock might be too much for Mrs. Nolan."

Now that he was leaving, Samantha felt she could relax a bit. She turned around and regarded him with her head tilted to one side. "Mrs. Nolan?"

"The receptionist."

A smile lighted Samantha's eyes. "Not to worry. That woman is unshockable."

He laughed, a rich, quick sound of amusement, and came to his feet. Without a pause he walked over to Samantha. With gentle fingers he brushed back wayward copper strands that had worked loose from her braid. "You have the most beautiful hair I've ever seen."

His hand cupped the side of her head. Alarm bells were going off in Samantha's brain like crazy, but she couldn't move. He had her trapped between his body and the cabinet.

"You're a blatant liar, Tobin," she accused, struggling to keep her words from jerking. "Nobody thinks red hair is beautiful."

He smiled slowly. "I do, and I'm a very discriminating man." His fingers strayed lower to brush the tip of her nose and lower still to trace the outline of her lips. "Your mouth is beautiful too. I've been wondering all morning how it tastes."

Samantha went stone still. The only thing moving in the room was Tobin's finger, tracing and retracing her bottom lip. She struggled to gather her scattered senses. She lifted her chin and curled her fingers around the edge of the cabinet top. "Like tuna fish, probably," she said.

"There's only one way to find out." He leaned closer. Samantha stiffened. "Relax, Samantha. You aren't afraid of me, are you?"

"No," she said steadily, lying through her teeth, "I'm not interested."

She saw a smile in his dark eyes. "We'd better do something about that."

"You could let me go, for starters." *Before I make a complete fool of myself,* she added silently. His fingers slid down to curl around the side of her neck. His mouth lowered toward hers, and she felt the warm flutter of his breath. It seemed suddenly that there was not enough oxygen in the room. Her lips parted as she took a deep breath.

His lips brushed hers as lightly as the touch of a feather. Or did she only imagine it? "Tobin, I want . . ." The objection trailed off as his lips brushed hers again, the contact fractionally firmer this time. In unconscious invitation her tongue came out to moisten her trembling lips.

"I know," he whispered. He touched his mouth to hers again and heard his blood roaring in his ears. It took all his considerable control not to crush her against him. He didn't want to frighten her; he wanted her to relax and savor the kiss. Her lips were soft and she tasted of feminine sweetness, not tuna fish. When he felt her rigid muscles relaxing slightly, he touched the tip of her tongue with his, then took her full bottom lip gently between his teeth.

Pleasurable heat seeped into Samantha. It felt as

though her bones were melting, and there was a languid heaviness in her limbs. Her eyelids fluttered closed and she leaned against him. Assailed by a rush of sensations, she was incapable of thought.

His body was hard against hers, and his strong arms pressed her closer. His mouth savored hers, moving lazily and softly, enticing and drawing her breath from her lungs. He smelled faintly of the musky cologne she had noticed in the car, and more strongly of clean male flesh. She let her head drop back to better accommodate the deep, drugging kiss, and he murmured her name as though it were the most precious word in the language. She sighed, and he gathered her closer. Foggily, she was aware that her arms were curved around his neck, but she didn't remember having put them there.

Without her knowing how it happened, she was kissing him back, yearning toward him, aching with a sudden, desperate need. With an agonized groan his mouth left off gentle enticing and crushed hers, and she felt the hammering of his heartbeat as desire raged through him. His tongue plunged in search of the sweet delights of her mouth, and she responded.

Samantha felt the stabbing pain of a passion stronger than any she had ever known. It was as though some deep, secret part of her opened for the first time, and alien wants and needs came spilling out. She wanted to satisfy those desires, to forget caution and consequences and let her exploding emotions take over. Conscious for the first time of the naked hungers that inhabited her body, she was frightened. She knew that if she didn't stop herself, and him, she would never recover from what would happen. Once she let the barriers down, this man would conquer every tiny part of her before he was through. There would be no holding back, no secrets. She would be destroyed.

Panicked, she struggled to free herself. He held her close for another long moment, his lips clinging, not wanting to relinquish her mouth. At last he let her go, and she moved away from him. Tobin watched her in silence until she lifted her head and met his gaze. His eyes were opaque, and she couldn't read what he was thinking.

"Please, go," she said, her voice shaking and betraying the turmoil inside her, "and don't come back."

"I'll go, Samantha, but I can't promise not to come back."

The absolute conviction in his tone made her shiver. It was as if they were caught in a net, a net in which struggling to be free only entangled one tighter. She backed away from him. "I don't want to see you again."

Tobin spread his feet, as if to brace himself. "Some things were meant to happen, regardless of what we want," he said quietly.

"I don't buy that," she snapped. Deliberately she turned her back to him. There was absolute silence for a moment, and then she heard him leaving. She didn't move until she heard the front door close. Then she folded her arms across her breasts and hugged herself until she stopped shaking.

CHAPTER FOUR

"Waylon Rutger recommended you. He said you handle a lot of marital stuff."

The client was forty and fat, with small, glistening eyes that reminded Samantha of a wary beast. He was perspiring freely, sweat spreading dark circles on his shirt under the arms. She had disliked him on sight. The fact that Milt Marois had been sent to her by Rutger, the ambulance-chasing lawyer who still hadn't paid Samantha his past-due bill, was another strike against the man.

"What sort of marital stuff did you have in mind, Mr. Marois?" Samantha inquired dryly.

"My wife's fooling around with this wimp she works with. I want the goods on her."

Samantha doodled on a notepad. "Do you have evidence she's seeing another man?"

Marois shifted his bulk in the chair. "If I had evidence, I wouldn't need you. I want tape recordings, pictures, the whole schmear. That broad thinks she can put one over on me, she's got another think coming."

If Marois's wife was, indeed, seeing another man, Samantha couldn't find it in her heart to judge the woman too harshly. She stifled an impulse to show him the door without further discussion. "If you're planning to divorce her, tapes would probably be inadmissible in court."

"I don't care about court. Just get me the tapes, I'll take care of the rest."

How would he take care of it? Samantha studied his flushed, perspiring face. Would he use threats? Physical abuse? "How?"

He eyed her shrewdly. "Listen, JoAnn don't want a divorce. We got two boys, and I've always been a good provider. Besides, this guy ain't about to marry her, and she couldn't take care of two kids on what she makes. And I ain't gonna shell out for child support so she can run around with some prissy bookkeeper."

Samantha stiffened. Ex-husbands who refused to meet their obligations to their children were a sore spot with her. She'd seen too many destitute women in this office, trying to trace vanished fathers. "Surely you want to support your children, regardless of the troubles between you and your wife."

"The way I see it, JoAnn can't have her cake and eat it too. She gets a divorce, she's gonna have the devil's own time finding me to put the bite on me. Know what I mean? But that ain't gonna happen. Once I get evidence she can't weasel out of, she'll break off with this guy. She knows which side her bread's buttered on."

Samantha glanced at Billy Bob, who was pretending to be engrossed in the contents of the corner file cabinet. He gave her a pointed stare that said: *So the guy's a jerk, but we need the money.* Which she already knew. She was in no position to turn away clients, no matter how she felt about them personally.

Samantha sighed. "Why don't you try talking to her first? Private investigators aren't cheap, Mr. Marois." She ignored Billy Bob's alarmed cough.

"I already tried that. JoAnn claims they're just friends." He gave a snort of contempt. "I wasn't born yesterday." His chair creaked as he sat forward. He went on earnestly, "I thought of breaking the guy's leg or something, but he's the kind who'd slap a lawsuit on me. Those sissy types are always looking for somebody to sue. Know what I mean?"

Accepting the inevitable Samantha reached for a case form. "My fee is fifty dollars an hour plus expenses. I require two hundred in advance."

Grunting, he reached into his hip pocket and pulled out a battered wallet. He drew out four fifties and laid them on the desk. "When you use that up, you get back to me with what you have. If I think you earned the advance, I'll keep you on the case."

Don't do me any favors, Marois. Samantha bit her lip to keep from voicing the thought. She looked at the four bills, thinking of the answering machine she needed. Her pen poised over the case form she asked, "Where are you employed?"

"Dependable Moving Company. I drive a van."

"And your wife?"

"She's a secretary at Financial Savings and Loan."

"The other man's employed there, too, you said."

"Yeah. A loan officer, they call him, but he's just a glorified bookkeeper. Name's Lance Starer. Lance!" He laughed mirthlessly. "What kinda name is that for a man?"

"Is he married?"

"Naw. Probably can't find a woman of his own. Has to mess around with other men's wives."

"I'll need your home address and phone number and Starer's if you know them." Samantha continued to question him and fill in the case form. Finally she said, "That about does it for now, Mr. Marois."

"Can you start on it this weekend? I gotta drive to Chicago and back, so it would be the perfect time. When the cat's away . . . You know what I mean?"

Samantha shuddered. If Marois used that phrase one more time and gave her that sly look . . .

"We'll get started on it." She stood. "I have another appointment in five minutes, Mr. Marois. Will you be in town next week?"

"I'm taking Tuesday and Wednesday off. I'll be home."

"Fine. You'll be hearing from me."

As soon as Marois was gone, Samantha expelled a weary breath. "Can you believe that man?"

"He reminds me of the heavy in a Bogart movie," Billy Bob remarked. "Do you think he could be Sydney Greenstreet reincarnated?"

Samantha chuckled. "Poor JoAnn Marois."

Billy Bob nodded. "I thought you were going to be at the Fitzgerald estate all weekend."

"I am. I guess you'll have to take over the Marois case until Monday."

Billy Bob's head jerked up. His eyes bulged. "You mean it, Samantha?"

"I've decided to take a chance on you, Billy Bob. Don't do anything to make me regret it."

He grinned. "Don't worry about a thing. I know exactly what to do. But I sure could use that Tricky Fountain-Pen Tape Recorder."

"You'll have to make do with what we have," Samantha told him.

Billy Bob pondered for a moment. "You told Marois you had another appointment. It's news to me. Must be real hush-hush."

Samantha tucked the four fifties into her jeans pocket. "Not really. I've got an appointment at the electronics store to buy an answering machine."

"Hot damn! Things are looking up around here. I better get started on my case. I'll run downstairs and make a copy of that case report." He snatched it from Samantha's desk and loped out of the office, muttering about disguises. Samantha was amused by his excitement, yet she couldn't help worrying that she was turning Billy Bob loose on a case before he was ready. But it was Friday, and she was due at Eleanor Fitzgerald's the next morning. What other choice did she have?

Samantha arrived at the Fitzgerald estate at ten o'clock Saturday morning. Eleanor, in jeans and walking boots, greeted her cheerily and handed her a pair of binoculars. "Leave your car keys with Wilkins. He'll see that your things are taken to your room. We'll do a little bird watching in the preserve, and I'll show you where we found the dead birds."

Eleanor practically crackled with nervous energy. She really was amazing for a woman in her eighties. Samantha only hoped she could keep up with her. "Great. But I won't be using the room much. I brought a sleeping bag. I plan to spend the night in the preserve."

Eleanor pursed her lips. "I'm sure you know how to do your job, dear, but I wouldn't want you to put yourself in danger."

"That's not likely. Shooting birds is one thing, harming people is another."

They were walking toward the preserve, Eleanor setting a brisk pace. "You're probably right. Just the same we'll keep this little secret between ourselves. As far as my employees know, you're a friend of the family. They'll suspect the truth if they learn you're camping in the preserve. No reason they should find out, though. Mike and Howard are off this weekend, and Ben will be in the caretaker's cottage except twice a day when he checks the preserve."

"Where is the caretaker's cottage?"

"Just beyond the preserve, at the back of my twenty acres." The path widened so that Samantha, who had been following, could walk beside Eleanor. The older woman continued, "Are you sure you want to be out here all night?"

Samantha smiled at Eleanor's doubtful look.

"Positive. I'm looking forward to sleeping out. My uncle Sam used to take me camping. Those times are among my happiest memories."

"You were named for him?"

Samantha nodded. "He's my father's brother. He raised me after my parents were killed. Sam died ten months ago, and I miss him a lot."

"Watch that tree root, dear." Eleanor gestured with her binoculars. "Were you an only child?"

"Yes, and I've always regretted it."

"Hmmm," Eleanor mused. "You and Tobin seem to have turned out all right, in spite of being only children. I worry about Grant, though."

"Your great-grandson?"

"Yes. Tobin's bringing him for a visit this afternoon. He received the progress report from Grant's school this week. Grant's scholastic performance has been poor, and he and Tobin had a row about it. When I talked to Tobin yesterday, he was thinking of transferring Grant to a military school where he'd have a more structured environment. Tobin thinks Grant could learn self-discipline there." Eleanor shook her head sadly. "Personally, I believe that would be a mistake, since Grant is so opposed to the idea. I sometimes think if Tobin and Charlotte had had another child . . ." She shook her head again. "Well, I shouldn't be boring you with family problems."

Samantha was far from bored. Knowing that Tobin would be there that afternoon sent a little shiver of excitement through her. She hadn't seen him since he'd left her at her house four days ago, but the kiss they had shared still haunted her idle moments. She was curious about Tobin's son, and even more curious about Tobin's late wife. Yesterday Samantha had been in the library researching a potential client's background and had run across a folder full of newspaper and magazine clippings on the Fitzgerald family. From one of the clippings she'd learned that Charlotte Fitzgerald had been a member of an old Philadelphia family as wealthy and socially entrenched as her husband's. She had attended the right schools and belonged to the right clubs. Although there was no picture of Charlotte in the file, Samantha was sure she must have been beautiful. In short, Charlotte had been the ideal wife for Tobin Fitzgerald III. She would be difficult to replace, which probably explained why Tobin hadn't married again.

Samantha and Eleanor wandered all morning along the twisting paths through the preserve, stopping frequently to observe the varied species of birds. The six dead birds—three bluebirds, two egrets, and a bald eagle—had been found in all parts of the preserve.

"They started with the bluebirds," Eleanor said, "then came the egrets, and a week ago Sunday we found the eagle."

"Nobody heard the gunfire?"

"No."

"They must have used a silencer." Samantha thought for a moment. "Does there seem to be any significance in the order in which the birds were killed?"

"The particular type of egrets that were shot are rarer than bluebirds, and the bald eagle is the rarest of the three. I've wondered if that was by design. If so, I can't think why."

"Perhaps to heighten your concern. The eagle would presumably be more difficult to replace than the bluebirds. Do you have anything rarer than bald eagles?"

An anxious frown creased Eleanor's brow. "The whooping cranes. We've been keeping them penned."

"Good. There's a progression here, which means the killer's working by a well-thought-out plan. These aren't random killings. The killer wants something. Whatever it is, I'll bet he tips his hand soon."

A couple of hours later, when they returned to the house, Tobin was contemplatively sipping a martini in the library. He was wearing light-tan slacks and a chocolate-colored, open-collared shirt. The boy who slouched in an armchair next to the window wore jeans with a plaid western shirt and cowboy boots. Grant had Tobin's lanky build and forceful chin and nose. But his eyes were blue, his hair dark blond and shaggier than his father's. He must have taken his coloring from his mother.

Tobin stood as the women entered, and his eyes went immediately to Samantha. Grant came to his feet more slowly; his attention, too, was on Samantha. There was the hint of a smile in Tobin's eyes; Grant's were opaque and bleak.

Eleanor went straight to her great-grandson. "You've grown another foot since I saw you, Grant!" She hugged him and stepped back for a better look. "I'm sending a care package back to school with you full of fattening cookies and cake. You're too thin. How's your appetite?"

"He has the appetite of a horse," Tobin drawled. "It's just that he's growing too fast for his weight to keep up."

Grant had been smiling at his grandmother, but when Tobin spoke, his scowl returned. He would be a handsome man one day, Samantha decided, in a more rough hewn way than his father. There were good bones in his lean face, and his blue eyes were very dark and intelligent. His scholastic performance was clearly not the result of poor mental faculties. Boredom, probably, or rebellion. Samantha felt a stirring of pity.

"Grant, this is Samantha Preston. She's doing some work for me this weekend. Samantha, my great-grandson."

Samantha smiled. "Hi, Grant."

"How do you do, Miss Preston. My father told me you're trying to catch the person who's shooting Grandmother's birds." Grant stared a moment, then blurted out, "You don't look like a detective."

"I don't?" Samantha caught Tobin's wry look. "Why?"

"You're a girl." A blush rushed into Grant's face.

The boy's outlook was nearer to Tobin's than he realized. Samantha tilted her head. Tobin hadn't taken his eyes off her since she'd entered the room, and it was beginning to make her tense. "I think I've already had this conversation with your father."

"I'll go and tell Mrs. Duffy to serve lunch in

fifteen minutes," Eleanor interjected. "I'm famished, and I'm sure Samantha is too. If you'd like to freshen up, dear, I've put you in the first room to the left at the top of the stairs."

Samantha welcomed the chance to leave the room. "Thank you."

Lunch was served in a bright garden room that opened off the formal dining salon. They sat at a glass-topped table surrounded by wicker and greenery. Grant was on Samantha's right, Eleanor on her left. Facing her across the table Tobin watched her from beneath half-lowered, dark lashes. He wasn't an easy man to be around, Samantha reflected as she dipped into a pile of nutty chicken salad on a bed of spinach greens. She felt self-conscious, exhilarated, and confused all at once. She was reacting to Tobin's presence like a giddy adolescent. She reminded herself that she was there to catch a bird killer, not let herself be carried away by a foolish infatuation.

Samantha slid a furtive glance over Tobin's son, who had spoken only when spoken to since they sat down, and then only in monosyllables. Evidently he was still sulking over the row he'd had with his father. That aside, however, he didn't seem to be happy. Did he still miss his mother? Samantha knew what it was like to lose parents in childhood. There were feelings of anger, betrayal, and guilt. Being sent away from home to school might have added to Grant's confusion. Who mothered him now? Tobin's mother? One of the classy women he dated? Nobody? For the second time Samantha felt pity for the boy.

"Mrs. Duffy's grandchildren are coming to visit her this afternoon," Eleanor addressed Grant brightly. She had made several efforts to include him in the conversation, without much success. "Perhaps you can spend some time with them."

Grant's only reply was a put-upon sigh.

"I thought you liked Teddy," Eleanor said.

"Teddy's okay," Grant conceded. "It's Milly I can't take."

"Milly's fourteen," Eleanor said to Samantha, "a difficult age for a girl."

"Maybe Teddy and I can give her the slip," Grant mused halfheartedly.

"Don't be rude to her, Grant," Tobin said. "Surely the three of you can find something to do together."

Grant rolled his eyes. "Like what?"

Tobin glanced at Eleanor as if for a suggestion. When Eleanor hesitated, Samantha offered, "How about a game of touch football?"

Both Tobin and Grant looked at her as if she'd grown two heads. Grant groaned, "Milly doesn't like to get dirty."

"Maybe we could get her to loosen up," Samantha said.

"We?" Tobin echoed.

"Sure." She looked from Tobin to Grant. "What we need is a football."

Eleanor said, "There's one in the garage, Grant. You left it here last fall."

"Great," Samantha said. "We'll organize a game.

Grant, how about if you and I take on your father and the other kids? That is, if Mrs. Fitzgerald can spare me for an hour or so."

"You go right ahead, dear," Eleanor said. "Nothing's likely to happen in the preserve until after dark."

Tobin almost choked on a sip of water. "You're not serious, Samantha."

"Absolutely." Samantha winked at Grant, who was looking at her with a new respect. "I think he's afraid we'll clobber him."

Eleanor laughed delightedly and Tobin sputtered, "Would you care to place a wager on it?"

"Done! A dollar?"

Grant, whose shoulders had been slumped dejectedly, straightened up. "Yeah, I'll bet a dollar too."

"Oh, my." Eleanor chortled. "This is going to be interesting."

Tobin looked around the table, his eyes narrowing as they returned to Samantha. "It'll be a pleasure to take your money."

"Don't count your chickens," Samantha cautioned him as she buttered a wheat cracker.

Grant was actually smiling. "I hope you're better at games than the girls I know, Samantha." Clearly he was relishing the idea of beating his father.

"It's been a while since I played touch football," she admitted, "but don't worry. I'm in shape, so I'll hold up my end of things."

Tobin continued to gaze at her in a deep, searching way that left her disconcerted. He looked lean and hard in his brown sport shirt. She felt a flutter of desire and ignored it. This man was off limits.

Later, as they left the sun-room, Tobin fell into step with Samantha. "I'll get you for this," he muttered in a low voice.

Samantha flashed him a smile, feeling happy suddenly. "I'll ask your grandmother to referee, to make sure nobody cheats."

He raised one dark brow. "I always play by the rules, Samantha."

"Whose rules?"

"Mine."

Milly, an extremely well-developed fourteen-year-old, was wearing so much mascara Samantha didn't see how she could hold her eyelids open. *Fourteen going on twenty-one*, Samantha thought. Milly refused to play, explaining, "I'd get grass stains on my new dress. I'd rather stay in the house with grandmother and watch television."

The way Milly had been cutting her eyes at Tobin ever since her arrival, Samantha wasn't sorry to see the girl go.

Eleanor watched the game from a chair on the back terrace, cheering impartially for both sides. At first Grant tried to play hard enough for two people, obviously not convinced Samantha was tough enough to compete on an equal footing in rough-and-tumble action with three males. She quickly disabused him of any such notion.

They played until they were exhausted. The game was tied six to six. "Is anybody pooped besides me?" Teddy, a panting, freckled eleven-year-old, asked.

"Just one more play," Grant begged.

Samantha was beat, but she wasn't about to admit it. Grant threw the ball and somehow she managed to snag it and stagger toward the imaginary goal line between two trees. She heard footsteps pounding behind her and poured her last bit of strength into a dive over the line. She sprawled in the grass, and her pursuer sprawled atop her.

Struggling for breath she wriggled onto her back and looked into Tobin's dark eyes. "You're supposed to tag me"—she gasped—"not tackle me."

"I tripped." He was breathing almost as heavily as she, and his dancing eyes dropped to her mouth.

"Tobin, let me up!"

"I'd rather kiss you," he mused half to himself.

Although he hadn't wanted to play football, he'd joined in with good grace. He was very good at sports, something she should have suspected by the fit leanness of his body. He could also be very direct when he wanted a woman to know he was attracted to her. He continued to surprise Samantha. He could drop the polished manners and understated elegance when he chose to. Today he was not the man she'd met in the offices of Fitzgerald, Fitzgerald and Fitzgerald. Turning away his advances might be more difficult than she had anticipated.

Samantha could feel every hard line of his body pressing against hers. She could feel her pulse beginning to hammer, and for an instant she thought he was going to kiss her under the watchful eyes of Eleanor and the two boys. It would be foolish to deny that the idea appealed to her, and equally foolish to let it happen.

"We have an audience, Tobin," she said softly.

After another moment's hesitation he slid off her and helped her to her feet. "Every time I see you, I'm more certain than ever."

"Of what?" She tilted her head.

He was smiling, and it pulled at her. "Sooner or later we're going to make love."

How could she answer such audacity without sounding either rude or coy? she wondered as she brushed grass off her jeans. Perhaps no answer at all would be best.

Grant came running up. "Grandmother says you were over the line, Samantha. Besides, tackling is illegal, Dad."

"He claims he tripped," Samantha said, tossing Tobin a wry glance.

"Anyway, we beat 'em!" Grant said.

"We sure did." Samantha stuck out her hand. "Pay up, Tobin."

Grant thrust his hand forward as well. "Me too."

Tobin slapped a dollar bill on each of their palms and muttered, "I knew I shouldn't have agreed to this."

Grant grabbed his dollar and ran back to the terrace to crow to Teddy and Eleanor. Tobin and Samantha followed more slowly. "You made his day," Samantha said. "Isn't that worth getting creamed?"

"No."

Samantha laughed. "You aren't a sore loser, are you, Tobin?"

"I don't know." His hand settled against the small of her back for an instant, then fell away as they reached the terrace. "I rarely lose."

CHAPTER FIVE

The moon was rising between the branches of a sycamore tree. Samantha spread her sleeping bag on a grassy spot she'd chosen that morning while birdwatching with Eleanor. Quietly she placed her flashlight and .32 automatic in its zippered case close at hand and stretched out on her back on top of the bedroll. Dressed in jeans and a long-sleeved shirt, she wouldn't need additional covering until the night was farther along.

She put her hands behind her head and stared up at the leafy sycamore branches. The bleaching light in the spaces between the leaves made a crazy-quilt pattern. The long-drawn-out hoot of an owl drifted over her, part of an eerie night chorus carried on the soft stir of air.

Now that she was alone and unoccupied, she could think about the extraordinary day. Tobin and Grant had still been in the house when she'd gone upstairs. Grant wanted to spend the night, but she didn't know whether Tobin had agreed to let him. In any case she'd heard Tobin's car leaving as she'd crossed the back terrace and entered the preserve.

Samantha had not been alone with Tobin since those few moments at the end of the football game. She'd made certain of that. She'd spent most of the afternoon with Eleanor, who had thanked her for instigating the game. "I don't think Tobin has roughhoused with Grant in years. Between you and me, I've been worried that my grandson was turning into a stodgy old bore like his father. Today was good for both of them."

Eleanor's description of her son made Samantha chuckle. "Does Tobin's father know you consider him a stodgy old bore?"

Eleanor grinned like a mischievous child caught in a naughty prank. "Oh, yes. I've told him often enough. Poor Toby. He made a dreadful mistake in his choice of a wife. I tried to tell him it was wrong, but he couldn't see it. So I made up my mind to do everything I could to like Rose, but she made that impossible. Rose has never forgiven me for advising my son not to marry her. At the moment she's trying to convince Toby that I'm getting too senile to live here alone and should be put in a retirement home."

Samantha laughed aloud. "You've got the sharpest mind of any woman I know, regardless of age. What makes your daughter-in-law think you're senile?"

Eleanor shook her curly head. "Perhaps it's Rose's way of getting back at me, after all these years. I've never understood how the woman's mind works. She's such a snob, and my 'common blood,' as she calls it, embarrasses her. Once when she was particularly angry with me, she said that blood always tells in the end. 'You can't make a silk purse out of a sow's ear,' is the way she put it."

Noticing Samantha's shocked look, Eleanor went on, "Oh, it's true enough. I was a housemaid when I met Tobin's grandfather, T.G. We eloped to avoid the furor that we knew would come if we announced our intentions beforehand. The marriage scandalized Philadelphia society for months. My husband's mother went into seclusion for a year until it died down. She lived for fifteen years after that, but I was never invited into her home. T.G. refused to go without me, so his relationship with his mother was effectively broken. I was sorry about that, but there was nothing I could do. His father was more tolerant. I think the old buzzard actually came to like me before he died."

Samantha listened to Eleanor's reminiscences with growing admiration. "It must have taken a lot of courage to defy your husband's family."

"For T.G., yes, although I didn't understand that at the time. I couldn't believe a mother would react as my husband's did, though T.G. tried to warn me. In the long run she was the one to suffer from her attitude; she lost her son. I, on the other hand, was extraordinarily lucky. I adored T.G. until the day he died, and he felt the same about me. The fact that he was wealthy and I was poor had nothing to do with it."

Eleanor's description of Tobin's mother had hardened Samantha's already formed conviction that she couldn't let the way Tobin made her feel overcome her good sense. He both attracted and unsettled her, and Samantha wasn't accustomed to being unsettled by a man. The few romantic relationships she'd had in the past had started with friendship and shared interests. All the men in her past had been easygoing, and willing to let her set the tone and pace of the relationship.

Tobin was in another category. Their life-styles could not have been farther apart. She wasn't even sure she liked him. She didn't think she understood him, and she was certain he didn't understand her. His intelligence drew her, but his highhandedness put her off. In spite of the many opposites in their personalities, both were accustomed to being in control. That she couldn't seem to overcome her physical attraction to him continued to surprise and disturb her. He intruded into her mind, even when her thoughts should be on her work, and she didn't like that.

The snap of a twig shattered her troubled reverie. Instantly alert, she sat up and reached for her gun. The sound the zipper made as she eased the case open seemed incredibly loud in the silence.

Quietly, she got to her feet, waiting. She heard the crunching sounds of footsteps through a bed of leaves. She released the safety catch on the pistol and edged backward until she felt a tree trunk at her back. Maneuvering around it she positioned herself so that the trunk provided a shield for her body.

The footsteps grew louder, coming closer. Suddenly they halted. "Samantha." Though the deep voice was low, it carried clearly.

She stepped from behind the tree. "Tobin?" she hissed.

The footsteps resumed, and a moment later a dark male form emerged from the trees. Tobin shrugged a bundle from his shoulder and tossed it to the ground.

Samantha approached to stand beside her bedroll, one hand on her hip. "What are you doing here?" she demanded in an angry whisper. "Do you realize I could have shot you?"

"My God, you have a gun?"

Samantha snapped the safety catch back in place and stooped to return the pistol to its case. "Would you keep your voice down!" she whispered. "Of course I have a gun—and a license to carry it. I'm a private investigator, in case you've forgotten."

He bent and began tugging at the bundle he'd dropped to the ground.

"What are you doing?"

"Unrolling my sleeping bag."

"Your *what?* Don't tell me you just happened to have it with you!"

"No. I drove to town and bought it, after Grandmother told me of this crazy scheme of yours to spend the night in the preserve. What do you plan to do if you actually catch a trespasser?"

"Use my gun, if I had to," she snapped, forgetting to whisper.

He shook out his bedroll and spread it beside hers. "And probably end up shooting your own foot."

His high-and-mighty manner infuriated Samantha. "I happen to be a crack shot, and I have the trophies to prove it!"

He straightened, surveying her moon-drenched face across the space of two sleeping bags. "How many people have you shot at?"

"I resent being subjected to the third degree, Tobin," she sputtered.

"Stop evading. How many?"

She stuck her hands in her pockets and glared at him. "Well—none, actually. But I've shot at plenty of targets. Besides, if the bird killer puts in an appearance, I'll only use the gun to frighten him."

"You little fool. Don't you know you shouldn't carry a gun unless you're prepared to use it?"

"I never said I wasn't prepared to use it. I'll aim over his head. If that won't stop him, I'll try for a flesh wound in the thigh."

"If you ask me, your whole plan is idiotic."

"Nobody asked you! Now, you can just pick up your sleeping bag and go home."

For answer he sat down on his bedroll and propped his arms on his drawn-up knees. "I'm not about to leave you out here alone."

Samantha dropped to her knees, facing him. "I hate this kind of macho stuff! I am quite capable of taking care of myself. I don't need a protector."

"I'm staying," he retorted stubbornly. "I couldn't live with myself if I left and something happened to you."

"Spare me the Sir Galahad act." Fuming, Samantha unzipped her sleeping bag and tossed the top half back. His tone was adamant; further argument would be useless. She lay down. "If you're going to stay, keep quiet. Our voices probably carry a mile."

She stared at the branches overhead. She heard him settling into a prone position on his bedroll. She could feel his gaze upon her, but she ignored it. She was unaware that he had edged closer until she heard his soft whisper in her ear.

"Samantha, why are you so nervous?"

His breath was warm against her cheek. "This is a stakeout," she hissed, irritated with his perception. "I could find myself in a confrontation with somebody carrying a gun at any moment. I'd be nuts if I weren't a little nervous."

"I didn't think detectives let a thing like danger bother them," he murmured. He reached out and twined the loose end of her braid around his finger.

She kept her arms stiffly at her sides, pretending not to notice what he was doing. "Good detectives are more cautious than other people. It's part of the job."

"I'm relieved to know you aren't planning to take any unnecessary chances." He raised himself on one elbow and a smile played over his face. His hand moved to her throat.

"Look, Tobin—" She struggled to remain perfectly still.

"Relax, Samantha. I'm not going to seduce you."

"Wow, that's a big load off my mind," she returned caustically. Her pulse hammered. She could feel the stirring of desire in her stomach, as his palm caressed her throat. "Or it would be, if I were naive enough to believe it."

"You can believe it, Samantha," he murmured. He wanted her. The urge to explore the soft secrets of her flesh was strong in him. He wanted her to expend herself, loving him, with the enthusiasm she'd had in the football game that afternoon. If he had ever wanted a woman so badly, he couldn't remember. "I won't seduce you," he whispered, his fingers stroking her throat, "because I won't have to. We strike sparks off each other. The mere sight of you arouses me, and your reaction to me is as strong."

"Whether or not we attract each other is beside the point, Tobin." With very little warning the sharpest sexual yearning she'd ever known filled her. "I'm working for your grandmother."

"Surely you get a break to relax now and then. I've been wondering. . . ." His voice was as soft as silk, and it trailed over her nerve endings as gently as his fingers. "Have you thought about that kiss at your house?"

"No."

He chuckled, his voice a low rumble in her ear. "I don't believe you. I've lain awake nights, thinking about it."

"That's your problem."

"I've even found myself thinking of you when I'm in the middle of a business conference." His fingers strayed to the open collar of her shirt and explored the hollow at the base of her throat. "It surprises me. Ordinarily I find the practice of corporate law totally absorbing."

"I'm sorry if your work's been affected." Her whisper was frail and unsteady, and that frightened her. "I don't want you to think about me. At the office or anyplace else." She was beginning to tremble from the erotic caress of his fingers, and she pulled away. "Whatever we feel, we can never do anything about it."

"Why?"

"Because you're—I'm . . ." She trailed off, rattled and more frightened than ever. She rarely found herself in a situation that she couldn't handle. She had always felt on an equal footing with men, had never been at a loss for words. "Because our worlds are too different. *We're* too different. You wouldn't feel at home with my life-style, and I couldn't stand the demands of yours. I think you know that as well as I. You're making it difficult for me to do my work, Tobin. If you insist on staying, please don't distract me."

Sighing, Tobin lay back and stared into the shadows. She was right, of course. They were from different universes, and the fact that they had met at all was the sheerest accident. He was what his social class had made him—bound by rituals he had never questioned, a conservative Philadelphia lawyer in the traditional sense. She seemed to know nothing of tradition. She constantly surprised him. He suspected she operated more on emotion than intellect. She carried a gun, for God's sake! But in this instance she made perfect sense. By all logical standards he shouldn't be attracted to her. She was nothing like the women he had desired before. He would like to believe it was only the novelty of her that intrigued him, that familiarity would breed disinterest, if not contempt. But somehow he doubted that. *Why couldn't he get her out of his mind?*

He heard her stirring and raised himself up on one elbow. She was taking her gun from its case. "I'm going on a short foray," she whispered.

"Did you hear something?"

"Shh. No. I just want to look around. Be right back." She crept silently along the dark path, and he let her go.

He lay in the darkness, waiting for her to return. As the minutes passed, he became more and more worried. Finally he decided to go in search of her. As he was setting out, he heard her returning.

"What are you doing up?" she whispered.

He flopped back down. "I was going to look for you. I was worried."

She put her gun back in the case. "That's ridiculous. I'm the one with the gun." She stretched out on her bedroll. "I checked the caretaker's cottage. The lights are on, and I saw Ben inside. Then I checked the sheds and the whooping cranes. Everything's okay."

His patience had gone with his peace of mind. "If they kill every damn bird in the preserve, it's not worth risking your life over."

"I'm not risking my life, Tobin, I'm doing my job." Her voice was soothing and calm, but he caught the amusement in it. "Stop nagging, okay?"

He swore as he rolled on his side. His chest brushed her shoulder. "Samantha, don't you think it's a bit childish for a grown woman to run around tracking down criminals, like Nancy Drew?"

So that's what he thought of her chosen profession. She turned her head and gave him a long look. "There are some who think it's as useful as what you do, Tobin."

"What the hell does that mean?"

"I don't see anything socially redeeming about finding loopholes in the law, so big corporations won't have to pay their fair share of taxes."

"Under certain circumstances that could be considered a legally actionable statement."

Her sense of justice was aroused, and she didn't care how angry she made him. "Forget the legalese," she countered furiously. "When you strip away the fancy offices and the big words, that *is* what you do!"

"Are you telling me I'm dishonest?"

"I'm telling you that people who live in glass houses shouldn't throw stones."

"Oh, damn! Did anyone ever tell you you have a naive outlook on life?"

"I care more for people than corporations. If that's naive, I plead guilty. So sue me."

Her innocent indignation moved him, and the fire went out of his anger. He was silent for a long moment, then a sigh escaped him. He lifted a hand to cup her shoulder. "I think you care more for *animals* than corporations. I'll bet you vote a straight Democratic ticket too."

"Is that an actionable offense as well?" She started to wriggle away from him, but his grip tightened.

He smiled. "You're a warm, compassionate woman, and lovely even when you're being prickly. It's difficult to hold your politics against you. Nobody's perfect." He bent his head to nuzzle her ear.

"Don't do that, Tobin." The preserve seemed suddenly far from civilization, and he was too close. She could handle the arrogance of the lawyer, but not the gentleness of the man. "I can't resist you when you're this way."

"I know." He lifted his head. The moonlight turned her face to alabaster, and her eyes were as dark and deep as jungle pools. "I find it very arousing."

"That's probably just male ego."

"Probably."

He lowered his mouth to taste her. The contact set Samantha's pulse drumming wildly, and she gripped his shoulders as if to steady herself in a world that had slipped its moorings. Then, just as abruptly, her fingers relaxed, and she wound her arms around his neck and parted her lips. She was a giver by nature, and recently there had been only her animals to give herself to. Now she gave to Tobin—all the sweet softness that had been imprisoned inside her for too long. Somewhere in a distant corner of her mind she knew she was already in love with him. *You're a fool. He'll break your heart.* She pushed the warning aside to be dealt with later.

"I want to feel your hair in my hands," he murmured as he released the clasp that secured her braid. He combed his fingers through it and buried his face in the loosened tresses. "It smells like honeysuckle." His mouth returned to hers to taste again, then wandered over her face. "I don't know what to do about you, Samantha. I desire you more than I ever desired anyone or anything."

The unsteady timbre of his voice undid her. His mouth claimed hers again, and the male taste of him invaded her blood, her body, her heart. He pulled her hard against him, and she was soft and pliable in his arms.

Even before his hands began to roam over her, her body was clamoring for his touch, her skin flushed, the nerve endings sensitive and needful. She knew there would be regrets later, but right now she only wanted more of his taste and the hard pressure of his body on hers. Her fingers buried themselves in his hair as she wound her arms more tightly about him. Then, with restless need, her hands ran over his shoulders and down his back, feeling the power in the taut muscles. She wanted his power, as well as his gentleness. She wanted every part of him.

She trembled when his hands slid beneath her shirt and unfastened her bra. He cupped her breasts, and her soft moan of pleasure filled his seeking mouth. This total swamping of her senses was new to her. There was a touch of insanity in it, but she wanted to feel more of it, to feel as she never had before, to lose herself in him. She wanted to beg him to take her quickly and stop this mad roller-coaster ride. Or would she never find her way back to solid ground and reason? *Never* . . . It was a terrifying word.

She pulled away abruptly and pushed his hands from her body. She stared at his face. Its angles were exaggerated by the moonlight. She fought to slow her quick breathing and felt the same painful struggle in him.

"I can't let this happen," she whispered huskily.

She expected denial, arguments, but instead he said, "I understand, but you're only postponing the inevitable. We can't fight what we feel indefinitely."

"We can try." She took a deep breath and felt her mind gaining control of her emotions once more. "We have to try." She moved to the far edge of her sleeping bag and curled on her side with her back to him.

Shaken by the violence of his feelings Tobin lay awake for a long time. Had he gone crazy? What was he doing here, trying to find a comfortable position in this miserable sleeping bag? He hated camping out. Another of the innumerable differences between him and Samantha. The irony of it was bitter in his mouth.

Samantha was more like Eleanor than any woman he'd ever known, and there were times when Eleanor's independence—her kookiness—nearly drove him mad. Yet his grandfather had lived with Eleanor for forty-five years. Tobin could remember when he first realized, as a teenager, that Eleanor and T.G. were the only couple he knew who epitomized the phrase *made for each other*. Their mutual love and respect had been extraordinary. But Tobin wasn't sure he was enough like his grandfather to cope with Samantha. She would never fit into his world. Oddly, he didn't want her to; if she did, she wouldn't be Samantha. It would be like caging a wild bird. He had gotten himself into an impossible dilemma, and he had no idea what he was going to do about it.

Samantha pretended to sleep, but her thoughts were racing. She must be demented, she told herself, to have allowed that scene with Tobin to happen. She had enough intelligence to know that, while Tobin might have an affair with her, he could never see her as anything more than a temporary pleasure. Coming out here to spend the night in the preserve was only a lark to him, a break in his real life at the office and the elite Philadelphia social functions. Was he silently laughing at her right now? She could hardly blame him if he were.

Thank goodness she had come to her senses in time. She vowed not to forget again the vast chasm of background, wealth, and privilege that separated them. She was the one who would be hurt if she deluded herself into believing that there could be anything important between them.

After chasing her troubled thoughts in circles she had finally fallen into an exhausted sleep. She didn't awaken until dawn. She scrambled to her feet, ignoring Tobin's sleepy question about where she was going, and ran to the pen where the whooping cranes were kept. To her horror one of the cranes lay on the ground. She let herself into the pen. The crane was stiff; it had been dead for some time. Frantically, she searched its body for a bullet wound, but there was none.

She ran to the house. Eleanor was already having her first cup of coffee in the garden room. She listened to Samantha's report and called her veterinarian, who arrived within the hour. He autopsied the dead crane in one of the sheds in the preserve, removing some corn kernels from its stomach.

"We never feed them corn," Eleanor said.

"I'd bet my reputation that these kernels are poisoned," the veterinarian said. "I'll send them to the lab, but I'm ninety-nine percent certain."

Seeing Samantha's stricken face Eleanor said, "It isn't your fault, dear."

But Samantha couldn't let herself off so easily. She brushed past Tobin, who had grimly watched the autopsy with them. She went to fetch her sleeping bag. Tobin followed her.

"Grandmother's right. You couldn't have stopped what happened."

She whirled on him furiously. "I might have, if I hadn't forgotten why I was here. This is as much your fault as mine! You shouldn't have come here last night!"

His jaw hardened. "You didn't feel that way a few hours ago."

Being reminded of the fool she'd made of herself only fueled Samantha's anger. "I don't want you to follow me here again. Find somebody else to amuse yourself with. I have a job to do, and you're getting in my way."

CHAPTER SIX

Monday morning Samantha went directly from the Fitzgerald estate to the office. The veterinarian had found a lab worker who came in on Sunday to analyze the grain the dead crane had ingested. The vet's diagnosis had proved correct; the grain had been poisoned. Both Samantha and Eleanor had been virtually certain that the bird killer wouldn't chance another incident that weekend, but Samantha had insisted on spending Sunday night in the preserve anyway. Tobin accepted her decision to continue the stakeout alone with poor grace; he took Grant home Sunday morning. She had spent most of the night patrolling the preserve, using a flashlight only when the darkness was so deep that she couldn't see where to place her next step. She was certain that nobody else entered the preserve, and after a thorough check Monday morning, she confirmed that no birds had died during the night.

She reached the agency office at nine-thirty. Billy Bob wasn't there, and from all appearances he hadn't been there since Friday afternoon. Probably so wrapped up in the Marois case that he didn't know what day it was, Samantha reflected. She felt a flicker of worry over his absence, deciding she'd better try to run him down if he didn't appear by noon. She spent a few minutes freshening up in the tiny bathroom adjoining the office before she checked the new answering machine for messages.

The first message was from Billy Bob. "Samantha, I hope you're sitting down. I've been arrested. I tried to tell these stupid cops I'm a detective, but they keep saying they've heard that one before. Can you come down Monday morning and vouch for me? If you don't, they'll probably leave me to rot in jail. It's a real bad place, Samantha."

Samantha slumped back in her chair, overwhelmed by her bad luck. She should have known better than to put Billy Bob on a case. At the time it had seemed her only choice. The Fitzgerald case took priority, but thanks to her inability to curb her feelings for Tobin, she'd bungled that too. All in all it had been a disastrous weekend.

Sighing, she flipped the answering machine back on and listened to a message from a young, struggling attorney who wanted her to dig up some information in courthouse records. She decided against getting back to him immediately; it would have to wait until she'd dealt with the police. There were no other messages on the machine. She set it to record again and left the office.

Fortunately the officer on duty at the station desk was Joe Harvey, with whom she'd shared information in the past.

Joe greeted her with a friendly wave. "What's up, Sherlock?"

Samantha took the nearest chair before she replied. The loss of sleep the night before was catching up with her. "You have my assistant locked up, Joe. What will it take to get him out? I don't want to call a lawyer unless I have to."

"What'd he do?"

"I was hoping you could tell me."

Harvey rifled through the piles of papers on the desk. "Name?"

"Billy Bob Digby."

"Digby—Digby—yep, here we are." Harvey pulled a sheet from the mess before him and began to read. "He ever been in trouble with the law before?"

"A couple of speeding tickets, I think."

Harvey looked up. "How well did you check this guy out before you hired him?"

"Well enough."

"You're sure Digby's never been hauled in on a morals charge before?"

"Before? No! Look, Joe, he's actually my secretary, and a good one. But he wants to be a detective, so last Friday I gave him a case to work over the weekend because I had to be somewhere else. He must have gotten carried away. What's he charged with?"

"Following a woman by the name of JoAnn Marois home from work, hanging around her house after dark, and window peeking. The Marois woman's convinced he was planning to rape her."

Samantha groaned. "JoAnn Marois's husband, Milt, hired my agency to find out if his wife is having an affair with another man. Billy Bob wouldn't harm a fly. It's all a misunderstanding."

Harvey leaned back in his chair. "JoAnn Marois might have been wrong about Digby's intentions, but she has a legitimate beef on several counts." He shook his head sadly. "Samantha, you better send this kid to detective school—or wherever you people learn your trade—before you let him investigate anything else. Sam Spade he ain't."

"Does that mean you'll release him?"

He thought about it. "I can probably get him out on your recognizance. He'll have to agree to stay in town for now, and he'll have to go before a judge if the woman decides to press charges." He smiled wryly. "Maybe she'll transfer her wrath to her husband when she finds out why Digby was following her."

"Do you have to tell her?"

"Not immediately, but if she wants to press charges, we'll fill her in. Wait here. I'll see what I can do."

Harvey returned ten minutes later with forms for Samantha to sign. Billy Bob followed the officer sheepishly. Samantha didn't even look at him. After signing the forms she clutched her handbag and walked out. Billy Bob followed at her heels.

"You wouldn't believe the types they have in those cells," Billy Bob informed her. "It's a snake pit. It's a wonder I'm still ambulatory."

"You're breaking my heart, Billy Bob."

He peered down at her. "You mad at me, Samantha?"

Samantha pushed through the station's glass double doors. "Why, no. I always gnash my teeth like this."

"Aw, Samantha, I'm sorry," he said miserably. "I just wanted to prove I could handle a case. I guess I was a little overeager. Maybe I'm not quite ready for investigative work yet."

They had reached Samantha's car. "I'd say that about sums it up, Billy Bob."

He sulked all the way to the office. Once there he threw himself into secretarial chores. Samantha spent most of the day investigating JoAnn Marois. When the woman left work, Samantha trailed her at a safe distance. JoAnn Marois was a frail, mousy woman who looked incapable of deceiving anyone. She went home and didn't leave again. Neither Lance Starer nor anyone else came to the Marois house. At nine o'clock Samantha called it a night. Tomorrow she would do some checking on Starer, but she was already half convinced that JoAnn Marois wasn't having an affair with anyone. If she hadn't found any evidence to indicate otherwise by Wednesday, Milt Marois would probably fire her. If he didn't, she would quit. After seeing JoAnn Marois, she was sorrier for her than ever. She didn't want to dig up any incriminating evidence against the woman, even if it existed.

When she let herself into the house, Churchill was barking furiously in the backyard. Samantha went straight to the kitchen and dished up dog and cat food, then fed the animals in the backyard.

"I'll let you come in later," she promised Churchill, "when I'm ready for bed."

She was half undressed when the telephone rang.

"Samantha?" It was Eleanor Fitzgerald. "I'm so glad I've finally reached you."

"I was out of the office most of the day," Samantha said, realizing that she had forgotten to call in before five and ask Billy Bob for her messages.

"I know. I talked to that nice young man who answers your phone. He said he'd tell you to call me the minute you returned."

"I didn't get back to the office. I hope you haven't found another dead bird."

"No. But there was a message in my box when Wilkins got the mail this afternoon. There's no postmark, so it was evidently placed there by somebody besides the mailman. We can't see the box from the house, so it could have happened almost anytime today."

"Is it typed or handwritten?"

"Neither. They've cut words from newspapers and magazines. Let me read it to you." She paused, then read, " 'If you don't want any more birds killed, you will cough up fifty thousand dollars in unmarked bills, small denominations. You will be notified later when and where to deliver money. If you are smart and follow instructions, you will not be bothered anymore. Do not tell police.' That last sentence is underlined twice."

"Have you told anyone else about this?"

"Oh, no, dear. I wanted to talk to you first. I'm willing to pay the money to stop the slaughter of my birds. I think we should do as they ask. What do you think?"

"I agree. At least, we should appear to be following instructions. Don't let anybody else see that note. I'll be out first thing in the morning."

"All right, Samantha. Good night, dear."

When Samantha finally fell asleep, she slept soundly. Refreshed, she arrived at the Fitzgerald estate at eight-fifteen the next morning. Eleanor received her in the garden room and insisted that Samantha join her for breakfast. While they ate, Samantha examined the ransom note. The words appeared to have been clipped from several different newspapers and magazines. They were glued to a sheet of cheap, lined paper, the kind used to make children's school tablets. Tracing the author of the note by tracking down the source of the tablet or the newspapers and magazines from which the words were clipped would be impossible.

"Does the expression *cough up* remind you of anyone?" Samantha asked.

Eleanor shook her head. "I can't think of anybody I know who uses it consistently."

"I didn't think so," Samantha mused. "That would be too easy. Our letter writer is too clever for that. The careful way he chose the birds that he would kill indicates a pretty shrewd mind. He knows something about birds, how endangered the various species are." Samantha hesitated, trying to think of a tactful way of asking the next question. "Mrs. Fitzgerald, how has Ben been behaving lately? Has he come to terms with his retirement?"

"I don't know," Eleanor said. "He hasn't said much about it since the day I told him I was going to retire him. He was angry when I told him and tried to argue with me, but I stood my ground. The work is too much for him now. Once his retirement is an accomplished fact, he'll find things to occupy himself with. He'll forgive me eventually."

There was simply no tactful way to put it, so Samantha said flatly, "He could be killing the birds to get back at you."

"No." Eleanor's denial was emphatic. "Ben has worked for me for forty years. He's always been loyal and trustworthy. More to the point he loves the birds and animals in the preserve. If he wanted to get back at me, he wouldn't do it this way."

"I'll need to question him anyway," Samantha said, "and the other caretakers too."

"I understand," Eleanor said. "They'll have to know what you've been doing here. Perhaps your questions will help them remember something that will be useful to you. All I ask, Samantha, is that you handle Ben tactfully. He's set in his ways and as independent as a hog on ice."

Ben was also a man who spoke his mind, Samantha discovered, when she interviewed the caretakers. All three were working, cleaning out one of the sheds, when Samantha found them. Mike and Howard greeted her in a friendly way; Ben mumbled a hello while regarding her with narrowed eyes.

"I'm checking into the trouble you've been having in the preserve for Mrs. Fitzgerald," Samantha said. "I'm a private investigator."

Clearly, they were surprised. Howard recovered his voice first. "You mean you're—like a detective?"

"That's right," Samantha said, "and I have Mrs. Fitzgerald's permission to ask you a few questions. Have you seen anybody in the preserve during the past two months who had no business here?"

Mike and Howard looked at Ben, who leaned against his shovel handle, still scrutinizing Samantha. "I haven't," Howard said finally. "Have you, Mike?"

"No."

"We're only here three hours a day, though," Howard went on.

"We have to work to pay our college expenses," Mike added.

Ben muttered, "Poor folks have to shovel out bird coops or whatever else they can do to get along in this world. You might say people like me, and these two boys here, are at the mercy of rich folks, like those up at the big house. No Fitzgerald ever had to sling manure to put food on the table. Nobody ever told one of them that he was no use to anybody anymore. It ain't fair, but that's life." The old man picked up his shovel and shambled out of the shed, still grumbling about life's injustices.

Samantha and the two young men stared after him. Finally, Howard said, "Ben doesn't mean to be rude. He's just old, and I don't think he's been feeling well lately."

"Has he said anything to you about his retirement?" Samantha asked.

"He told me Mrs. Fitzgerald was pensioning him off," Mike replied. "Ben was pretty mad about it. He was insulted that Mrs. Fitzgerald didn't think he was able to do the work he used to do." Mike grinned. "She's right, but I wouldn't tell Ben that."

"Evidently he resented my questioning him," Samantha said.

"He hasn't said anything about seeing anybody in the preserve," Mike said. "But I'll ask him again when he's in a better mood. I'll tell Mrs. Fitzgerald if he remembers anything. Sure beats me why anybody would risk sneaking in here to kill birds. Maybe it's some kid, trying out a new gun."

"And feeding the whooping cranes poisoned grain?" Samantha asked.

"Yeah, there's that." Mike's expression was perplexed. "I don't get it."

Samantha talked to the two young men awhile longer, but learned nothing to aid her in her investigation. She left them her card, asking them to contact her if they noticed anything suspicious in the preserve. Going back to the house she reported the gist of her conversation with the caretakers to Eleanor.

"There's nothing more I can do here now," Samantha said finally, "so I'm going back to the office. Let me know the minute you hear anything else about the ransom."

She drove back to town, pondering Ben's obvious resentment of Eleanor and the Fitzgerald family.

Shortly after she arrived at the office, Joe Harvey called from the police station. "I've got bad news and good news," he told her.

Samantha glanced at Billy Bob, who was busy at his typewriter, and sat down behind her desk. "Tell me the good news first. I could use some."

"Mrs. Marois has agreed not to press charges against Digby."

She covered the receiver with her hand. "Billy Bob, JoAnn Marois isn't going to press charges!"

Billy Bob's drawn face shifted and took on the look of a man rescued from the gallows at the last minute. "Whew!" He swiped imaginary sweat from his brow.

"Thanks, Joe," Samantha said into the phone. "What's the bad news?"

"To get her to drop the charges I had to tell her that Digby was working for you and that her husband had hired your agency to investigate her activities."

"Oh, no," Samantha muttered. "Well, it couldn't be helped. Thanks for warning me, Joe."

Did JoAnn Marois have the nerve to confront her husband with what she knew? Samantha wondered about that for the rest of the day, finally deciding that the woman looked too timid to confront Milt Marois about anything. Tuesday morning she learned how wrong she was. Her first telephone call of the day was from Milt Marois.

"What kind of detective agency are you running

down there?" Marois shouted into the phone. "I never heard of such a bunch of stupid incompetents! JoAnn's threatening to leave me for spying on her!"

"Mr. Marois," Samantha interjected, "I'm sorry my assistant wasn't more discreet. I've been checking on your wife myself, and I don't think she's having an affair with anyone."

"What do I care what you think! You're fired!"

The slamming of the receiver on the other end of the line echoed in Samantha's ear as she hung up. She would have relished telling Marois she was quitting, but he hadn't given her the chance. Sighing, she considered going to the courthouse to do the research on the new case, but decided to put it off another day. She didn't want to be out of the office when Eleanor called. So far there had been no further word from the blackmailer, but Samantha was sure he would make contact soon. Until he did, she would find it difficult to settle her mind on anything else for very long.

But Eleanor didn't call. Samantha stayed at her desk until six before she gave up her vigil for the day. Her neck was taut from the tension of waiting. She rolled her head back and forth to loosen the muscles as she locked the agency door behind her. The blackmailer was evidently going to draw out the suspense so that when he finally did make contact, Eleanor would be frantic enough to agree to his terms. Clever. Or just mean, Samantha reflected as she thought about Ben's resentment of Eleanor. The old caretaker would know, better than anybody, how much Eleanor cared for the birds in her preserve. He would realize that keeping her worrying over what he would do next would be an effective punishment for her "injustice" to him. Samantha had phoned Eleanor last night to suggest that she tail Ben for a day or two—perhaps she'd be lucky enough to catch him putting another note in the mailbox. Eleanor wouldn't hear of it. "I won't do anything else to hurt Ben's pride," Eleanor insisted. "Besides, I refuse to believe he's involved in this."

On the way home Samantha stopped at the supermarket; dusk was graying the horizon by the time she stopped her car in front of the house. Lugging a full bag of groceries in each arm she hurried up the walk, head down. Just before she reached the front steps, she looked up—and came to an instant halt.

Grant Fitzgerald was sitting on the bottom step. He was wearing the same faded jeans and cowboy boots he'd worn on Saturday, with another western shirt. Next to him a guitar was propped against the steps.

He tried to grin jauntily, but the grin faltered half-formed. "Hello, Samantha." He looked so forlorn, it brought a lump to Samantha's throat.

Grant was in some kind of trouble, something so bad he was afraid to go to his father or grandmother. What other explanation was there for his turning up on the doorstep of somebody he barely knew? *Be careful how you handle this, Samantha,* she cautioned herself. "Well, hi," she said lightly. She handed him her keys. "Unlock the door for me, will you?"

He stared at her. He'd probably expected her to react with shock or anger. He scrambled to his feet. "I can carry those."

"No, I'm okay. Just unlock the door, please." He retrieved his guitar and clambered up the steps. Churchill was barking furiously.

"His bark's worse than his bite," Samantha said as she entered the house ahead of Grant. "Be quiet, you old fraud," she said to the dog. "It's only me and my friend Grant." She went straight to the kitchen. Grant followed her, with Churchill sniffing at his heels. Finally satisfied that the stranger was okay, Churchill flopped down on his belly and watched Samantha put away the groceries. Occasionally, he whined dolefully to remind her that it was dinnertime.

Samantha handed Grant a can of dog food. "We'd better feed him before he gets really pitiful. There's a can opener in the top drawer, and his bowl is on the back porch." When Grant returned to the kitchen, Samantha asked casually, "So, what are you doing in my neighborhood?"

He spread his legs as if bracing for a fight and announced defiantly, "I've run away from home."

"I see." Samantha eyed him calmly as she got eggs from the refrigerator and began breaking them into a large mixing bowl. "You've picked a pretty poor place to run to. I'm not much of a cook. Dinner is cheese omelets and bran muffins."

"That—that's fine," he stammered, while continuing to watch her warily.

"Okay, you can set the table and pour two glasses of milk."

She was aware of Grant's watchful gaze as she finished making dinner. When they were seated at the table, he blurted out, "Dad wants to send me to a military school. I don't want to go, but he doesn't pay any attention to what I want!"

"So you decided to run away," Samantha commented. "That should get his attention."

"Are you going to tell him I'm here?"

"Not right this minute. Tell me something, Grant. Do you like your present school?"

"Not really."

"Is that why you aren't applying yourself to your studies?"

He frowned and buttered a couple of muffins. "I guess so."

"You know, it isn't easy to be the only parent in a family. Your father's probably very worried about you. Maybe this military-school idea is a desperation move. What would you do in his place?"

"I'd listen to what my kid had to say, for one thing."

Samantha studied him. His omelet was gone, and he was on his fifth muffin. She'd forgotten about adolescent appetites. As he ate, he scowled.

"Suppose he did listen," she said finally. "What would you tell him?"

"I want to live at home. I hate that dumb boarding school. There are good schools in Philadelphia. I don't see why I can't go to one of them."

"I imagine your father feels you wouldn't have enough supervision at home. He's a very busy man."

"I don't need to be supervised," Grant grumbled. "I can take care of myself."

Samantha smiled. "You probably can, but you have to understand that it may take a while for your father to accept it. Parents worry. It's the nature of the beast."

He rolled his eyes. "Tell me about it."

They looked at each other in a moment of sympathetic understanding. Then Grant finished off the last muffin. "Want some chocolate ice cream?" Samantha asked.

"Maybe later. Right now I'm stuffed."

He wandered into the living room while Samantha put the dishes in the dishwasher. She heard him strumming his guitar softly. Joining him a few minutes later she settled in the cane rocker. He started to put the guitar aside, but she said, "No, don't. Play for me." She put her head back against the chair and closed her eyes.

He began to play a mournful tune. After a few moments he sang softly. The song told the story of an unhappy wanderer who was looking for "a place that felt like home."

"That's nice," Samantha said when he finished. "What's the name of that song? I don't believe I've ever heard it before."

He flushed. "I haven't thought of a title yet."

"You mean it's your song? You wrote it?"

"Yeah."

"Why, it's beautiful, Grant. You're very talented."

"Do you really think so?"

"Absolutely."

"That's what I'd really like to do when I finish school," he confided. "Write and sing my own songs." His face reddened again. "I guess you think that's pretty dumb."

"Why would I think that?"

He shrugged. "Dad says a lot of people want to be singers, but most of them don't make it."

Samantha knew she shouldn't contradict his father, but she couldn't help saying, "That's because they give up too easily. You can be anything you want to be, if you're willing to pay the price."

He gave her an odd look, then scrunched down on the couch. He yawned hugely. "Gosh, I'm tired. I walked around for hours before I came here."

"You take the room at the end of the upstairs hall. The bathroom's right next door."

He straightened up. "You mean I can stay?"

"For tonight, anyway."

"Thanks, Samantha." He picked up his guitar and walked to the stairs. Halfway up he turned back. "Samantha."

"Hmmm?"

"You're the neatest girl I ever knew."

She grinned. "Thank you, Grant. I like you too."

She puttered quietly in the kitchen until she was sure he was asleep. Then she phoned Tobin's house. Tobin himself answered. There was a harried note in his voice.

"Grant's with me," Samantha said. "He was sitting on my front steps when I got home."

"Don't let him take off again. I'll be right there."

"He isn't going anywhere. I fed him, and he's

103

gone to bed. Can't you leave him alone until morning?"

There was a moment of tense silence. Then he snapped, "No," and hung up.

CHAPTER SEVEN

Samantha studied him. Tobin had finally agreed to have a cup of coffee before storming upstairs and waking Grant. She had filled two mugs, and now they sat at her kitchen table speaking in low tones. The table was illuminated by the soft glow from the control panel of the electric range. The only other light in the house came from a reading lamp in the living room.

Tobin gripped his mug in both hands, his shoulders hunched forward. He frowned into his coffee. His curtness on the telephone had come from his deep worry over his son. When she'd opened the door to him a few minutes earlier, his drawn face and rumpled hair had been evidence enough that he'd been going through hell since Grant's disappearance that afternoon. Since it was a school holiday, he'd left Grant asleep when he went to work that morning. A servant had phoned his office shortly after noon to tell him that Grant was nowhere to be found. Tobin had rushed home and, after questioning the servants and scouring the neighborhood, had called everywhere he could think of that Grant might have gone. Shortly before Samantha's call he'd contacted the police. Now that he knew Grant was safe, he was understandably angry.

"I don't think you should wake him," Samantha ventured. He took a swallow of coffee and lifted his abstracted gaze to her face.

"It's obvious you don't have any children," he muttered. He released his grip on his mug long enough to rake both hands through his hair, rumpling it further.

"That's true," she agreed, "but on the other hand, maybe I can be more objective than you."

"He's had his family in a state of panic for hours. He has to be made to understand what he's done." Tobin gripped his mug again, frowning. "Thank God I decided to wait until morning to tell Grandmother."

"Yes, that's a blessing." Eleanor was under enough strain, waiting for word from the blackmailer. At her age learning of the disappearance of her grandson might have been too much to handle. Samantha gazed at the wet ring left by her mug on the table. "Did you notify the police and your parents that Grant's safe?"

He expelled a deep breath. "I called them before I left the house." His mother had insisted that stern disciplinary measures were called for "before Grant brings disgrace on the family." It had angered him that she seemed more concerned with preserving the family's image than with the fact that Grant had been found unharmed; but he'd told himself that people react differently under pressure. Besides, he'd agreed with her, though for other reasons. A military school where rigid discipline would be imposed looked more and more like the best solution to his problems with his son. "Why did he come to you, did he say?"

She ran her finger idly around the rim of her mug. "I think it was a case of his having nowhere else to go. I suppose he thought I could be counted on not to overreact, since I'm not a member of the family."

"Is that what you think I'm doing?"

"Since you ask, yes." She met his steady look. "He told me you're going to send him to a military school."

"I don't know what else to do. His last report card was abominably bad."

"Even knowing he would hate it? I'd say that's an overreaction to poor grades. And it will probably guarantee even worse grades in the future."

"Dammit"—he stared into the shadows for a moment, then took a deep breath—"you may be right. He just might be failing deliberately to spite me, though why he wants to, I don't know. At any rate I can't understand that kind of self-destructive behavior."

"It's the only weapon he has, Tobin."

His mug stopped halfway to his mouth. "To use against me? Why does he need a weapon? I'm his father."

"And he desperately needs your love and approval."

Frustration blazed in his eyes for an instant. "He knows I love him. As for my approval, he seems to be doing his darndest to make sure he doesn't get that."

"I think that's the point. He wants to feel that you won't reject him, no matter what he does." An intensity had crept into her voice without her knowing.

He stared at her, moved by her passion. "I've never rejected him." She looked at him without reply, but there was compassion in her eyes. "What are you thinking, Samantha? Tell me."

"It's really none of my business how you raise your son." Samantha got up to refill her mug. Restlessly, she wandered to a window before coming back to the table. "But I'm going to say it anyway. The very fact that you put him in a boarding school is a rejection in Grant's eyes. He wants to live at home with you. Tobin, I know what it's like to feel cast adrift, unwanted. My parents died when I was ten. I understood that they had died in a car accident, but I still felt rejected and abandoned. Then I went to live with my uncle Sam, but his wife didn't want me. I had no one to talk to, no one to help me understand the confusion in my life." She took a deep breath. She hadn't meant to reveal so much of herself to him, but it was impossible not to make comparisons between Grant and herself at that age.

He looked bewildered. "I thought it would be good for him, that he'd be better off away from home after Charlotte died. I thought new surroundings would help him get over the loss of his mother." Her eyes searched his, and what she saw encouraged her. He loved his son very much. She reached out to touch his hand. "But that was the very time when he most needed to be with you. I know you did what you thought was best, but Grant must have felt he had lost both his parents. Maybe he thought you blamed him somehow for his mother's death. Children's logic is sometimes quite convoluted. Grant is still a child, Tobin. He needs his father's love and acceptance with no strings attached. Just love him, without conditions."

He looked down at her hand, which lay lightly on his wrist. Musing, he lifted it and studied the slender fingers. "Thank you."

"For what?"

He linked his fingers through hers and looked up, a small frown of concentration creasing the bridge of his nose. "For stopping me from going upstairs when I was angry," he said quietly. "For being honest." He smiled faintly. "Though I doubt that you know how to be any other way."

Touched, she gripped his hand tightly. "You'll wait until morning to talk to him, then?"

The simple warmth of her touch moved him deeply. After a brief hesitation he nodded. Still in the same musing tone he said, "When Charlotte died, I had no idea how to deal with an eight-year-old boy alone. It would seem I deluded myself into believing that my convenience and Grant's needs were one and the same."

"It was a traumatic period for you too. That's never a good time to make important decisions."

"How did you get so smart in so short a time?"

The bemusement of his expression sent warnings ringing in her brain. In her urgency to defend Grant she had exposed too much of herself to him. He had come too close to the essential reality of her. If she let him in, she would never be free of him. "I took smart lessons, Tobin," she said glibly. She pulled her hand free of his and rose to wander to the darkened window again. Taking a moment to compose herself she turned and smiled at him.

"Don't do that."

She arranged her face in a mask of innocence. "What am I doing?"

"What you always do when I get too close. You run for cover."

She studied him. "I've no idea what you're talking about."

He came to his feet slowly. "Yes, you do."

Neither of them moved. Then, with a little shiver of trepidation, a feeling of disaster barely avoided, Samantha walked out of the kitchen. After a moment Tobin followed her into the living room. She was sitting on the couch, her legs folded beneath her.

"I want you, Samantha."

She looked up at him, her eyes large and vulnerable. "I know."

"You want me too."

Desire trickled through her bloodstream, as hot and potent as though he held her in his arms. "It isn't that simple, Tobin." A spring night chill seemed to have invaded the room suddenly. She pulled an afghan over her and let her head fall back against the couch.

"Why isn't it?"

She closed her eyes. *Because I've fallen in love with you*, she thought. *Because you would possess me totally. And when you walked away, you would take my heart and soul with you, and the pain would finish me.* "Tobin," she said softly, "don't make this more difficult for me."

She heard him moving to the couch, and when she opened her eyes he sat down beside her. "*You're* making it difficult, Samantha."

She heard the intent in his voice and drew a shuddery breath. "I have to—if I let you love me . . . I—I don't think I could deal with afterward."

His hand came to rest on her shoulder, and her muscles tensed. "You can trust me not to hurt you." He bent and brushed her forehead with a kiss.

Her heart hammered in her chest as she fought the growing, aching need. "You wouldn't mean to." Her voice was unsteady. "But you would. It's inevitable." His hand moved to cup the back of her head. She could feel a heaviness growing in her limbs. "Don't." She started to stand, but he caught her in his arms.

He looked intently into her eyes, brows drawn together. "I don't understand you." He planted brief, gentle kisses on her brow and cheek and at the corner of her mouth.

"Please, Tobin." Samantha knew that if he didn't stop very soon, she would be lost. Already she could feel her resolution slipping. Needs, longings, panic, were flooding in on her. "Let me go."

For a moment his grip tightened. God, he needed her. He looked into her green eyes and thought he might drown there. But it was their vulnerability that made him hesitate, then reluctantly release her.

"Thank you," she murmured, and got to her feet. She headed for the stairs. On the landing she turned back around. "I'm very tired. Good night, Tobin. You may sleep on the couch if you want. If you leave, be sure you lock the door behind you."

"All right." He watched her ascend into the darkness at the top of the stairs. His mind was a confusion of emotions and half-formed thoughts. She was dismissing him, and he felt rather foolish. Had her eyes really held vulnerability a moment ago?

She managed to get to her room and shut the door before her tears spilled over.

Surprisingly, she slept almost the moment she got into bed, her tears drying on her cheeks. It might have been minutes or hours later when she awoke from a dream of being locked out of her house by her Aunt Ruby who had come to claim the house as her own. Panic stricken, Samantha had pounded on the door, but Ruby wouldn't admit her.

The instant she awoke, she was aware through some sixth sense that she wasn't alone in the room. She blinked and peered into the dimness. She sensed as much as saw him.

"Tobin?" she murmured, her voice thick with sleep.

He was standing beside the bed. For the past few minutes he had been watching her sleep, touched by the childlike innocence of her face in the light from the hallway. "Samantha." He kissed the top of her head. How did she manage to become more beautiful every time he looked at her?

"What are you doing in my room?"

"Trying to decide whether or not to wake you. You cried out in your sleep."

"She locked me out." Samantha remembered the fear of abandonment she had felt in the dream, and tried to clear her head.

"Who?"

"Aunt Ruby." She yawned and rubbed her heavy-lidded eyes. She had been deep in sleep and still felt so sluggish that merely moving was an effort.

He sat down on the bed and settled her in the crook of his arm. "Your uncle Sam's wife?"

She rested against his shoulder. "Ummm. She took over my house and wouldn't let me in."

A forlorn note had crept into her voice, though he doubted she was aware of it. The feelings of rejection suffered by the child were still a part of the woman. Tenderness swept over him. "It could never happen," he said huskily. "Churchill wouldn't stand for it."

She smiled and touched his cheek. "Thank you. I hadn't thought of that." She settled more comfortably against his shoulder. It would be so easy to fall asleep again, sheltered in Tobin's arms. Her eyelids drooped. "You're a sweet man, Tobin," she murmured. "I didn't know that before."

The ache of desire trembled in him. "Your hair always smells like honeysuckle," he said. His mouth grazed her brow lightly, warm and tantalizing.

"That's my shampoo." She rested her head in the crook of his arm to look up at him. His mouth was waiting for hers.

His lips settled on hers and found them soft and defenseless. She stirred in his arms and he felt her drowsiness leaving and wariness taking its place.

"Tobin." Samantha's eyes flew open. "You shouldn't be in my bed." The warm strength of him felt too cozy and inviting. "I hardly have any clothes on."

"Yes, I know." He nuzzled his mouth against her throat, feeling her pulse leap in response as her fingers dug into his shoulders. He trailed his fingers over her shoulder and down her breast. "You feel wonderful." Her nipple hardened between his fingers. "Let me love you, Samantha."

"Oh, Tobin." She had never felt so defenseless in her life. The churning, demanding need was overwhelming. "We can't. Grant's at the other end of the hall."

"Don't worry about Grant. When he goes to sleep he's dead to the world. An earthquake wouldn't wake him."

She stared at him, her whole body throbbing with love for him. "It would be such a mistake."

"How can anything that feels so right be a mistake?" His mouth returned to hers. How he wanted her! He had never known such wrenching desire, not even with his wife. It pounded in his blood, clamped down on his muscles and bones.

Maybe she was right, but he was too far gone for it to matter.

Samantha knew that she was incapable of giving only a part of herself. If she let this happen, she would give everything. She was more aware than he realized of the frightened child deep inside her. More than anything she needed to belong to somebody. That need went deeper than physical desire and would be there even after the other was satisfied. "It isn't fair," she whispered with her final degree of opposition.

In silence Tobin gazed into her eyes, his hands still molded to her flesh. She was incapable of sending him away; he saw it plainly in her soft expression. He would see that she had no regrets; he made that a solemn vow to himself and to her. Had he had the strength, he would have walked from the room and left the house. All he could manage to do was to force his hands to fall from her body. With a little sigh of reprieve she leaned back against the pillow.

"Samantha, I need you more than I ever thought I could need anyone. Don't send me away, please."

If he had tried to make demands or to take advantage of her weakened defenses, she might have been able to say no. But she couldn't turn away from his humble admission and the plea that was as strong in his eyes as in his words. With a helpless little murmur she put her arms around him.

In a rush of pent-up emotion, his mouth possessed hers desperately. He crushed her to him with such convulsive strength that, a moment later when his mind caught up with his body, he feared he had hurt her. She felt small and fragile in his arms, and he cautioned himself to be gentle. But there was no gentleness in him, nor did she seem to want gentleness. She had made her decision and she would not go back.

With trembling hands he tugged her filmy nightgown up over her waist and shoulders and tossed it aside. Her hands, as eager as his, urged him to shed his clothing.

They fell together on the bed. Samantha felt such pleasure that she thought she would burst. His body was hot and hard with the desperate urgency that coursed through him. She felt his need and reveled in it. Time was suspended, golden, glittering, and it was enough right now that he needed her and that she wanted to give herself. She ceased at that moment to be an abandoned child or a fearful woman or anything else except the lover that Tobin's hungry kisses and fevered, roaming hands demanded that she be. She gave herself to him as a gift—completely, freely.

She wanted the pressure of his body on top of hers, the taste of him deep in her mouth. She became the aggressor, kissing him feverishly and running her hands over his body until he could bear no more and thrust deep into her.

Her body arched against his until everything beyond the boundaries of their flesh spiraled into oblivion. Her hungry mouth drank in his taste, her hands molded against the small of his back to urge him deeper. The flavors and textures of him made up the whole of her universe.

Tobin felt his control shredding. He wanted to hold back, and continue the slow, easy rhythm that was making her moan his name softly, to keep on feeling her shudder beneath him, to know that she belonged to him utterly. But he had to relinquish the straining remnants of control or go mad. Then he could no longer think or do anything but lose himself in her.

For Samantha the moment was one of total abandon followed by drowning waves of pleasure. In the aura of contentment that lingered after their loving, there was no room for regrets. Samantha curled against him, drifting in the most complete contentment she had ever known. Tomorrow would be time enough to think of consequences.

She awoke the next morning with no memory of having stirred during the night. A movement of her arm told her that Tobin had left the bed. How long had he been gone? Where was he?

She dressed quickly in a cotton skirt and blouse, tying her hair back with a ribbon. She found Tobin and Grant in the living room.

Before she could speak, Tobin said, "I came for Grant. I hope you don't mind my coming in and waking him, Samantha."

She took her cue from him. Evidently Grant believed his father had arrived only that morning. For an instant her eyes locked with Tobin's. What was he really thinking? Did he have as many ambivalent feelings this morning as she?

"Of course I don't mind. How are you this morning, Grant?"

Grant, who was sitting in the cane rocker, his guitar over his knees, turned his head to look at her, his eyes full of accusation. "You called my father. You double-crossed me."

Tobin rose from the couch. "That's enough, Grant."

"No, please, Tobin. I can understand why he's angry with me." She faced Grant. "When you've had time to think about it, you'll realize I had no choice but to call your father."

Grant pushed himself out of the rocker. "Can we go now, Dad?" Without waiting for a reply he stalked to the front door.

Tobin's gaze held Samantha's for an instant before he said, "Yes, we'll go." Of Samantha he inquired quietly, "Are you all right?"

"Of course. I'm fine."

But she didn't believe it, even as she said it. Perhaps it they had been able to talk, but that was impossible with Grant there.

After Tobin and Grant had gone, she walked through the house, touching familiar objects reflectively as though she had never seen them before. But it wasn't her environment that had changed, it was Samantha herself. She had loved Tobin before last night, but now he completely possessed her—body, mind, and spirit. Oddly, she felt a prisoner in her own house. Yet she knew that it was really her own mind that held her prisoner.

She had made a terrible mistake, one that she would probably never recover from fully. After last night she would never be able to stop loving Tobin.

CHAPTER EIGHT

The night with Tobin crowded everything else from Samantha's thoughts. She spent the morning at her desk, trying to sort out her feelings about what had happened. Billy Bob asked her several times what was bothering her; after lunch she sent him to the courthouse for copies of several documents, just to get him out of the office.

The hours spent thinking helped to settle her anxiety. A calm acceptance took its place. She would not go back and change what had happened with Tobin, even if she could. She loved him, needed to be needed by him. It couldn't last; she'd known that from the beginning. When it ended, she would deal with the pain somehow. Although her conclusions came with an edge of melancholy, she felt in control of her life again.

Tobin phoned her at the office at four o'clock. She'd given up on hearing from him that day, and the sound of his voice almost brought tears to her eyes.

"How are you feeling?" he asked.

"Still a little stunned," she replied honestly.

He chuckled, and there was a note of relief in the sound. "I'm very grateful for last night."

Alone in her office she blushed. "The feeling is mutual."

He laughed again. "I want you so much right this minute, I'm thinking of canceling an appointment and coming down to your office."

She smiled softly. "That's not a good idea. My secretary will be back any time."

He drew a deep breath. "I'll have to be patient, then. Samantha?"

"Hmmm?"

"The things you said about Grant—you were right. I spent the morning with him. We really talked to each other, for a change, instead of at each other. I'm taking him back to school tomorrow. He's agreed to buckle down and pull his grades up. He'll finish the term there, and next year he'll live at home and go to school in Philadelphia."

"I'm glad you were able to talk to him, Grant. He's a pretty great kid."

"I never thought he wasn't, but apparently that's not the message I conveyed to him. Anyway, Grant and I would like to invite you to have dinner with us this evening."

She felt a thrill of anxiety. "At your house?"

"Yes. Grant wants to apologize for accusing you of double-crossing him. I just want to be with you."

"Oh, Tobin, I don't know. . . ."

"Please. Grant will think you're angry with him if you don't come."

Samantha knew that going to Tobin's house for

dinner was yet another step closer to him, and she had misgivings about it. Yet the idea pleased her too. Besides, she told herself, she should go for Grant's sake. "All right. What time?"

"Seven-thirty? I'll pick you up."

"No, I'll drive. See you then."

For the evening Samantha dressed simply in a lavender cotton scoop-necked sweater and a flared skirt splashed with lavender and purple flowers. She had denied an impulse to buy something dressy for the occasion. She couldn't afford it; also, she had made up her mind always to be herself with Tobin. She couldn't compete with the other women he knew, and she wouldn't make a fool of herself trying.

Tobin himself admitted her to the lovely old house. Some of Samantha's doubts dissipated when she saw he was dressed casually in cords and a cotton shirt.

Smiling, he drew her into the foyer. "Don't look so serious." He bent and gave her a quick, hard kiss.

"I can't help it. I almost didn't come." It was difficult to resist the attraction Tobin had for her at any time, but when he was smiling at her like that, it was impossible. She tilted her head and smiled back.

"If you hadn't come, I'd have hunted you down." He took her hand and led her into the living room—or sitting room, or parlor, or whatever one called such a room in a Gothic mansion. Samantha felt overwhelmed. Tobin lived with the kinds of things a wealthy sixth-generation Philadelphian inherits: ornate antique clocks, orange Fitzhugh porcelain, Aubusson-covered Louis XV chairs, pastels by Whistler, and oils by other old masters. Watching her reaction Tobin laughed. "What do you think?" He kissed her again.

"It's wonderful. I've never seen anything like it."

"You should see my bedroom," Tobin told her mischievously.

She smiled. "I don't think I could cope with any more at the moment."

Tobin reached out to touch her hair. "You're beautiful."

She might have thrown her arms around his neck if Grant hadn't appeared in the doorway. "Hi, Samantha."

"Hello. Feeling better?"

He came into the room. "Yeah. Dad says I can live at home next year."

Samantha nodded. "That's great!"

"Samantha, I'm sorry about what I said to you this morning. I know you did what you thought was right."

"It's forgotten."

Grant looked relieved, and Tobin said, "I think dinner's ready." He took Samantha's hand. "We're eating in the den. The cook didn't have much notice that a guest was expected, so it'll be something simple."

A white-draped round table had been placed near the den's large, leaded glass window. A uniformed houseman was arranging silver serving dishes on the table as they entered. Dinner was spinach salad, asparagus vinaigrette, and broiled sole. The houseman hovered in the background to keep Grant supplied with milk and Tobin and Samantha with Dom Pérignon. The crystal and silver reflected the room's soft lamplight. *I wonder what the cook would have come up with if she'd had time to get fancy,* Samantha mused wryly, as she tasted her sole. It was delicious.

After dinner Samantha asked, "Do you know what it would take to make the evening perfect, Grant?"

"What?"

"You playing and singing for us." She glanced at Tobin. "Grant has composed a wonderful song."

Tobin's brows rose in surprise. "Really?"

Grant shuffled his feet self-consciously. "May I be excused, Dad?"

"Certainly."

"You'll be back with your guitar, won't you?" Samantha asked.

"Oh, Samantha, I dunno—"

"Please. I really want to hear you play."

It took a lot of coaxing, but Grant finally agreed to play for them. When he returned with his guitar, Samantha settled into a softly padded sofa with Tobin beside her. She smiled encouragingly at Grant.

The boy strummed softly, a little awkwardly at first, aware of his father's attention. But as he played, he began to relax, his head bent over the guitar, lost in the music. The lamplight shone on Grant's hair, turning it to burnished gold. His face was young and vulnerable. He was so like Tobin in many ways. Samantha would have liked to reach out and touch Grant's cheek. He was a fine boy and he'd be a fine man. She wondered what it would be like to have a son of her own. She shook her head. She had to fight such sentimental thoughts, couldn't let herself become too attached to Grant.

Before he left them, Grant played and sang his own song, the one he'd played for Samantha at her house. When he'd finished, it was a moment before anybody spoke. Finally Tobin said, "That's good, son. Very good."

Grant beamed. He couldn't have been more pleased if he'd won a top country/western music award. After Grant had said good-night and gone upstairs, Samantha looked at Tobin. "You see? I told you how much your approval means to him."

"I have to admit he's got talent," Tobin said, but he was frowning.

"You'd prefer it if he had a tin ear, though, wouldn't you?"

Tobin's eyes were serious. "I can't honestly encourage him to pursue a career as an entertainer."

"Don't take a twelve-year-old's whims so seriously. Grant will probably change his mind about a career a dozen times before he's grown."

He put his hand on Samantha's shoulder. "I wish I could be more like you," he said quietly.

Samantha shook her head. "In what way?"

"You're able to go with the flow. I think you could probably cope with anything."

Samantha was astounded that Tobin saw her in that light. In reality there was too much in her life that she didn't know how to cope with—chiefly the way she felt about Tobin. She was amazed that he couldn't see it.

She felt his fingers sliding below the scooped neck of her sweater and took a deep breath. "Tobin . . ."

His other hand slid through the smooth, shining strands of her auburn hair. "When I opened the door tonight and saw you, with the wind blowing your hair, I thought you looked like a wood nymph," he murmured. "There's something so elusive about you, Samantha. Sometimes I think I've dreamed you up."

She laughed as the warmth created by his words rushed through her. "You're talking like a drunk man, Tobin. Did you have too much champagne?"

"It's not the wine." He drew her into his arms. "It's you." He gave her a long, deep, satisfying kiss that promised pleasure beyond imagining. "I like your hair loose like this. It feels like silk." His lips grazed her cheekbone. "I'm thinking about locking that door over there. Have you ever made love on a Portuguese carpet?"

"We can't." Samantha smiled and shook her head. "The servants would come to clear the table, and they'd know exactly what we were doing."

"It doesn't matter. They're very discreet." He kissed her again, lingeringly.

She couldn't be that nonchalant. She wasn't used to living her private life with other people tiptoeing in the background. She shook her head, drifting under the spell of his kiss. She didn't think she could ever get used to the way Tobin lived.

She drew herself away from him. "Not here, Tobin."

He bent to kiss the corner of her mouth. "It's time to show you my bedroom, then." He stood and reached out a hand to her.

She tilted her head to smile at him as she accepted his hand and came to her feet. "I sleep in my great-grandparents' bed," he told her. He slipped an arm around her and led her from the room and up a wide, curving staircase.

The bed was made of elaborately carved dark wood, its headboard almost as tall as the ceiling. On the wall next to the bed was an oil portrait of a bearded man with dark, piercing eyes.

"That's my grandfather, T.G."

"Eleanor's husband?" He looked very proper, not at all like the family rebel Eleanor had described. But then portraits of that era were almost always stiff and unnatural. Samantha smiled softly at Tobin. "You look a little like him."

"More than a little, Grandmother says."

He turned her to face him and put his hands on her shoulders. He kissed her temple.

"But you're not a rebel, like your grandfather," Samantha murmured. Her lids lowered as she drew him closer.

"I never thought so," he said quietly, "until recently."

She hadn't the sense at the moment to figure out what that meant. She could only lean against him and lift her mouth to invite his kiss.

Gently he lowered her to the bed. Samantha lost herself in the feel and taste of him. Her mind was flooded with love, her body flushed with desire. She belonged to Tobin completely. As he undressed her, and then himself, she gazed with growing wonder at the perfection of him. He was a strong man, self-confident as only someone of his background could be, shrewd and unyielding in business dealings, but to her he had shown a tenderness that she knew few people had seen. For tonight it was enough—more than enough.

His hands and mouth roused her slowly, until she was quivering for him as he was for her. From somewhere in the house came a faint murmur of voices—the servants clearing the dishes and locking up for the night. There was the smell of clean sheets and rich furnishings. The bedside lamp turned the dark red bed-hangings a deep, rich burgundy. Somewhere an open window admitted the scent of pine and lilacs.

Then the storm within them gathered and finally broke free. Samantha clung to him and rode the crest of the storm until it left her weak and sated.

"You're mine," he muttered as he gathered her limp body into his arms.

"Yes." She buried her face in his neck. For tonight, at least, it was true. She slept quickly, as deeply as an exhausted child.

Tobin lay awake, feeling her warm breath on his neck and the light weight of her against his side. He stared at the dark velvet canopy overhead, wondering, *What is happening to me?*

But he knew. Until last night he had convinced himself that once he'd had Samantha, he'd be able to get her out of his system. It had happened that way in the past, and he'd had no reason to think it would be otherwise with Samantha. How wrong he had been. After the past two nights she was so deep inside him that he could no longer tell himself she was remotely like the others.

He listened to her deep, even breathing for several minutes, but this was something he had to share with her. He turned to her and roused her slowly with kisses.

"Samantha . . . sweet Samantha, wake up."

She woke groggily with his lips lingering on hers. "What?"

"I have something to tell you."

"Mmmm."

"I'm falling in love with you."

She blinked, suddenly wide awake. She stroked his jaw tenderly. "That would be a mistake, Tobin."

"Why?"

"We're too different. Our worlds are too far apart."

"Details," he grumbled, not wanting to hear what she was saying.

"Your parents would never accept me. It would scandalize your friends. Think what that would do to Grant."

He held her tightly and buried his face in the auburn cloud of her hair. "All that matters is how we feel about each other."

Her hands stroked his shoulders and back. "You know that isn't all that matters. It would be naive of us to think so."

"You don't love me." His voice was so low she could barely hear it.

"You're wrong. I love you desperately, but it should never have happened." She had never meant to tell him. She had never meant to have any of this conversation. She went on, "Life isn't a romantic story, Tobin. We're too old to believe in fairy tales."

He was silent for a long moment. With her head resting against his chest, she could hear the steady beat of his heart. At last he tilted her chin and kissed her. "Tonight I can believe in anything. Here you are in my bed—warm and soft and incredibly lovely. It's my own private fairy tale."

Her heart began to skip erratically. Just for tonight she would let herself believe in it too—the once-upon-a-time part, if not the happily-ever-after ending. This time their loving was lazy and unhurried, lingering kisses and gentle touches and murmured love words. But when the end came, it shook them again with its power.

Samantha slept again, but lightly now, knowing that she must leave before anybody else was up.

Tobin slept in snatches. In between, his thoughts circled endlessly, never coming to a satisfactory conclusion. He loved this woman, and he'd been incautious enough to tell her so. That in itself astounded him. He wasn't an impulsive man. He could not remember a time before when he hadn't done what was expected of him, including marrying the right woman and, since Charlotte's death, dating more of the right women. Doing "the right thing" was the code by which he'd been raised and which guided his adult actions. He had known since childhood the path his life would take, had even felt smug in the knowledge. It had never occurred to him that there might be other, equally satisfactory ways to live until he'd met Samantha. She was the antithesis of what he had always believed to be his kind of woman. She had slipped beneath his guard and claimed his heart before he knew what was happening.

When, in a dark, predawn hour, Samantha stirred beside him, he had hit upon the rudiments of a plan. She sat up and slid her legs off the side of the bed. Tobin reached out for her and pulled her back into his arms. "I don't want you to go." He buried his face in her hair.

"I have to. Grant will be up soon. It wouldn't do for him to find me here." Rising, she dressed in the feeble light from a distant streetlamp. Glancing at his shadowed form she asked, "Did you sleep well?"

"No. There was too much to think about."

"Oh." She dropped her sweater over her head and pulled it down.

"I thought over what you said—about us. I think you're wrong. You *can* be a part of my world."

She smiled faintly. "That's only what you want to think."

"How do you know unless you try?"

She slid one foot, then the other, into her sandals, her head held to one side as though she were considering what he'd said.

He was encouraged. "Will you go with me to the symphony ball next week?"

She made a soft sound of amusement. "Balls aren't exactly my cup of tea, Tobin. For one thing I have nothing to wear."

"I'll buy you a gown."

Her back stiffened. "I'll buy my own gown—if I decide to go."

Her reaction didn't surprise him. Secretly he admired her stubborn independence. "When will you decide?"

She shrugged. "In a few days." She bent and touched his cheek with her fingers, a brief, somehow pensive caress. "Perhaps we shouldn't see each other in the meantime. I need time to think." Slowly she let her hand fall to her side and crossed to the door.

Tobin sat up in bed. "Samantha . . ."

"Good-bye, Tobin," she said softly. The door whispered shut behind her.

It would be a mistake to go to the symphony ball with Tobin, Samantha told herself over and over as the day progressed. Despite what Tobin wanted to believe, she would be horribly out of place among the members of Philadelphia society. She would give herself forty-eight hours to think about it, but she already knew what her answer to Tobin should be.

During the day's idle moments she armed herself with reasoned arguments to explain to Tobin why she couldn't accept his invitation. At three o'clock Eleanor Fitzgerald phoned and drove thoughts of the ball from Samantha's mind.

"I've received further instructions from that

person." Samantha didn't have to ask who "that person" was; Eleanor's emphasis on the words made them sound like an obscenity.

"Another note?" Samantha asked.

"No, this time he telephoned. He must have put something over the mouthpiece, because his voice sounded muffled."

"That could mean he thought you might recognize his voice if he didn't disguise it." Samantha thought again of Ben, the old caretaker. "On the other hand it could mean only that he's taking every possible precaution to keep from being identified. What did he say?"

"I'm to bring the money to an abandoned house on the outskirts of town. He gave me detailed directions. I took it all down. I'm to be there at midnight Saturday. Alone. He said to leave the money on the front steps and drive away."

"You can't go alone," Samantha protested. "It's out of the question."

"He said if I brought anyone with me or if I'm followed, every bird in the preserve will be killed. I have to follow his instructions, Samantha." Eleanor's voice crackled with anger. "I probably shouldn't even have called you. He warned me not to tell anyone."

Samantha shivered involuntarily, thinking of Eleanor going out to a deserted shack alone at night to deliver the money. If anything happened to Eleanor, Samantha would never forgive herself. Thank goodness Eleanor had decided to take Samantha into her confidence. "We'll make him think you're following instructions to the letter,"

Samantha mused. "By the time he knows otherwise, it'll be too late."

"What do you mean?"

"Sit tight. I have a plan. I'll be out there Saturday night."

CHAPTER NINE

Saturday night. A full moon and excitement edged by anxiety. There was always the possibility that something could go wrong, although Samantha didn't expect it. As she drove to the Fitzgerald estate, excitement was her predominant feeling. She had spent the past two days in the office and was ready for action. Tobin had honored her request to be allowed time to think and hadn't called her.

Tonight she had put that particular dilemma aside to concentrate on the job she was going to do for Eleanor Fitzgerald. She arrived at the estate about ten, saw that Eleanor had left the garage door open as requested, and parked beside the polished old Rolls. Carrying a shopping bag Samantha moved stealthily to the back door.

Eleanor opened the door before Samantha had a chance to knock. "I've been watching for you," Eleanor whispered. "The servants have retired. We have this wing all to ourselves."

Samantha slipped inside. "Good. I drove past the drive twice before turning in, to make sure I wasn't being observed."

Eleanor led the way to her bedroom. "I've laid out my brown suit. It'll blend into the darkness, and the jacket's loose and has big pockets."

Samantha examined the jacket. "This looks fine." She slipped out of her jeans and shirt and dressed in Eleanor's clothes, dropping her pistol into the jacket's deep pocket. "I brought my own leather walking shoes." Eleanor's shoes would be too small for her. Samantha took the shoes from the shopping bag and put them on.

Eleanor watched Samantha. Her expression was worried. "I'm having second thoughts about this, Samantha. All they'll need is one good look, and they'll realize it isn't me. Let me call Tobin. He can hide on the floor behind the backseat of the car. In case you need help."

"No," Samantha responded sharply. Tobin would never agree to let her go ahead with her plan. "My gun is all the help I'll need. I know what I'm doing, really. This is my job." She lifted a curly gray wig from the shopping bag. "Wait till you see me in this." She put it on. "What do you think?"

Eleanor studied Samantha and couldn't help laughing. "It looks almost exactly like my hair. How did you find it?"

"It wasn't easy."

Eleanor said reluctantly, "It might work, if they don't get too close or shine a flashlight in your face."

"We're about the same height and weight, and I'll make sure they don't get a good look at my face before I'm ready. It'll work." It had to. Samantha was aware that she was taking a risk, going to the meeting place without backup. But the man had warned Eleanor that he wouldn't show himself if he suspected she wasn't following his instructions to the letter. "Do you have the money?"

Eleanor nodded and pulled a key from her pocket. She unlocked a small antique cabinet and took out a canvas bag, its drawstring pulled tight. "Here it is. My banker got very uneasy when I told him I wanted so much in small bills. I finally had to remind him that I had every right to ask for my money any way I wanted it. I made him swear not to tell anybody about the withdrawal, especially members of my family. The poor man was sweating blood by the time I left, but he'll keep my secret."

"With luck you'll be redepositing the money Monday morning." Luck. It could break either way, Samantha knew, but she couldn't dwell on that. She'd worked out her plan, and she'd follow it. She took the money bag, surprised at how heavy it was. "Now the car keys."

After a brief hesitation Eleanor handed Samantha the keys to the Rolls-Royce. "It's only ten-thirty. There's time for a cup of coffee before you go."

Samantha sensed that Eleanor had still not fully accepted the idea of Samantha's taking her place; she feared for Samantha's safety. Samantha had to appear calm and in control, to reassure Eleanor. "Coffee sounds wonderful. It'll keep me alert." She grinned. "Not that I need anything. My adrenaline's moving at top speed as it is."

They drank their coffee in the kitchen. "You'll phone me as soon as it's over?" Eleanor asked.

"I'll be coming straight back here."

Eleanor shook her head. "The drive could take an hour. Don't keep me in suspense that long."

Samantha smiled. "Okay. I'll find a phone and call you before I start back. Try not to worry. All right?"

Eleanor nodded, but Samantha knew she might as well ask her not to breathe. Eleanor would feel responsible for whatever happened tonight. Samantha just had to make sure everything went according to plan; then Eleanor would have nothing to blame herself for later. They finished their coffee in silence, the atmosphere thick with Eleanor's worry.

A few minutes before eleven Samantha left the house by the back door, as quietly as she had come. She backed the Rolls out of the garage, reversed it, and drove slowly toward the main road, giving herself time to get used to the feel of driving the classic old car. Kept in tiptop shape by Eleanor's chauffeur, the Rolls's engine purred as quietly as a kitten. She drove at a sedate pace, the canvas bag containing the fifty thousand in the seat beside her; she didn't want to arrive at her destination early and have time to worry over everything that could go wrong. It was easier to remain self-confident if she kept moving.

She reached the abandoned house at ten minutes before midnight. *So far, so good,* she told herself as she carried the bag of money to the sagging front steps. She set the bag down, returned to the car, and drove away, resisting a desire to look back. She had to hide the car in a grove of sycamores a half mile down the road and make her way back to the house under cover of the trees bordering the road. She'd gone through a trial run the previous night, and it had taken eight minutes to get back to the house. That gave her a narrow, two-minute margin. If the blackmailer arrived earlier than that, she would go to Plan B and intercept his car as he drove back down the road. That would mean, of course, that she would have to use the Rolls to block his way, and she would have to force him out of his car. She didn't like Plan B; too many unknowns. She accelerated and turned the Rolls off the road and into the grove. She killed the motor and, after satisfying herself that the Rolls could not be seen from the road, headed back to the house. Visibility was better than she'd hoped for. Thank goodness for the full moon. Luck was still with her.

Her tension had reached knife-edge sharpness by the time she reached the perimeter of the trees, from which she could see the abandoned house in surprisingly complete detail. The money bag was still on the top step. Relief washed through her. She leaned against the trunk of an oak tree for a moment to catch her breath and get poised for the next step of her plan.

Five minutes passed, and Samantha began to worry. Had she come to the wrong house? Had the blackmailer realized she wasn't Eleanor Fitzgerald? Had he spotted her as she made her way back to the house through the trees? Did he suspect a trap? Samantha checked for the flashlight in her left pocket, then her right hand closed over the grip of her pistol. She waited, unmoving.

From the corner of her eye she caught the headlight beam of an approaching car and stepped behind the oak tree. The car came slowly into her line of vision and halted in front of the house. Nobody got out for several moments. Cautious cuss, Samantha thought grimly. Then, both car doors opened and two men got out and walked toward the house. Squinting, Samantha tried to make out the stooped form of Ben, the old caretaker. But neither of them was Ben. Their carriage and gait were that of much younger men. They wore dark clothing and caps pulled down low on their foreheads.

The taller of the two picked up the money bag. "Just like we told her. What'd I tell you?"

Something vaguely familiar about that voice, Samantha thought. The second man said something too low for Samantha to hear. And the first answered, "Shine the flashlight on it, and we'll make sure we've got the genuine article here and not shredded newspapers."

She hadn't counted on dealing with two of them, but it was too late to change her plan now. Where had she heard that voice before? Samantha stepped from behind the oak tree. She took the gun from her pocket, released the safety catch, and crept quietly toward the house. Suddenly, an overhanging branch caught in her wig and, with her next step, lifted it off her head. She halted and sucked in her breath. The wig had dropped somewhere to her left, but she couldn't risk taking her attention from the two men to look for it. It didn't matter now, anyway; they'd know she wasn't Eleanor Fitzgerald soon enough.

The men had the bag open now, and one of them was shining his flashlight down inside it. The other lifted out a packet of bills. "Would you look at that? Never expected to see that much money at one time in my life."

The other man laughed and flicked off the flashlight. "Let's get out of here. This place gives me the willies."

Samantha ran the next few steps to bring herself within fifteen feet of them, target range. She turned her flashlight beam on their faces, and they looked up, blinking and startled. She gasped as she recognized Mike and Howard, the two college students who helped Ben in the preserve.

She raised her right arm and leveled the pistol at the two men. "Drop the money, and get your hands up." She might have tried tying one man with her belt and delivering him to the police, but she couldn't handle two of them. She would have to take the money and send them on their way before she could return to the Rolls. But she could identify them for the police; they'd find them within twenty-four hours. "I said drop the money!"

Howard dropped the bag.

"Now, get your hands up!" She turned off the flashlight and returned it to her pocket. She needed both hands for the gun.

They put their hands on top of their heads.

"Hey, it's that lady detective," Mike drawled. He sounded relaxed, not like a man with a .38 pointed at his belly.

"I do believe you're right," Howard said. "Samantha, isn't it?" He took a deliberate step toward her. "Now, you wouldn't really pull that trigger, would you, Samantha?"

"Halt!" Samantha was sweating now.

"Naw, she wouldn't do that," Mike said. He began walking slowly toward Samantha. "All that blood. You couldn't live with two dead men on your conscience, could you, Samantha?"

Bracing her feet wide apart and leveling the gun, Samantha cried, "Stop or I'll shoot. I swear I will!"

Mike laughed and kept coming. She aimed inches above his head and pulled the trigger. The shot sounded like a bomb exploding in the still night. Mike and Howard dropped to the ground, unharmed but terrified.

Howard cursed, his voice quavering. "Don't shoot again. We'll do whatever—" He lifted his head. Samantha's ears rang from the gunshot. Over the ringing she heard the wail of an approaching siren. "Oh, hell," Howard groaned, "you had the police out there all the time. Why didn't you say so?"

"No, I—" As amazed as Mike and Howard by this turn of events, Samantha watched as a police car screeched to a halt.

Tobin leapt out of the backseat and raced to Samantha's side. He grabbed her, whirled her around, and peered down into her face. "You're all right? Thank God!" He hugged her tightly.

"What are you doing here?" she asked shrilly, shrugging his arms away. Seeing that the police were dealing with Howard and Mike, she engaged the safety catch and dropped her gun into her pocket.

"Grandmother called me. Fortunately she became frightened and decided to tell somebody what you were up to. I called the police and they picked me up on their way out of town." His tone had changed from scared to angry. "Are you crazy, Samantha? You could've been killed! When I heard that gunshot, I thought—"

"That was my gun you heard. They aren't even armed." She stalked away from him toward the police car, where Mike and Howard were being stuffed into the backseat by two burly officers.

Tobin followed her. "You didn't know they'd be unarmed when you embarked on this insane fiasco!"

Samantha ignored him. "Do you want me to follow you to the station, officer?"

"That won't be necessary, Miss Preston. You can come downtown Monday with Mrs. Fitzgerald, and we'll take care of all the paperwork then. Are you going back with us, Mr. Fitzgerald?"

"No, thank you."

As the police car drove away, Samantha trudged down the road toward the Rolls's hiding place. Tobin matched his long stride to hers. Neither of them spoke until Tobin finally demanded, "Why do you take these risks?"

"It's my job, Tobin. Will you get off my back?"

He bristled and didn't speak again until they had reached the grove where she'd left the Rolls. She parted low-hanging branches and switched on her flashlight to point the way.

"I'll drive," said Tobin behind her. "Good God, how'd you get it in here?"

"It wasn't easy," she admitted.

They got in, and Samantha turned off the flashlight. Darkness enveloped them. Tobin grunted. "I can't believe I'm involved in such an idiotic situation."

"And with such an idiotic woman?" Samantha shot back.

Tobin reached for her. "Don't put words in my mouth, dammit." He pulled her into his arms. She could feel the pounding of his heart, and the anger left her. Her arms crept around his waist and she buried her face in the hollow of his neck. "Samantha, Samantha . . ." He stroked her hair. "I was so scared on the drive out here. I kept seeing you at the mercy of criminals."

She tilted her head back. His features were lost in the darkness. "I was never in any real danger," she whispered.

"I've never known such a maddening, stubborn woman. If you'd been hurt, sweetheart—" He abandoned the terrifying thought as his mouth groped blindly for hers. The hands that cupped her face trembled. His fear for her safety hadn't fully left him yet. It was as if he were afraid to believe he actually held her, whole and safe. If she hadn't loved him before, she would have fallen in love with him at that moment. She pulled him closer and deepened the kiss.

"For a while tonight," he muttered against her lips, "I was terrified I'd never be able to kiss you again."

"Don't make me cry, Tobin." She kissed him slowly and felt his trembling fingers grow still against her face.

"You taste so good," he whispered, and planted soft kisses all over her face.

She smiled and her mouth went in search of his again. "Umm, you taste good too."

With a single movement he turned sideways on the seat and lifted her into his lap. "Are you still mad at me for showing up tonight?" His breath was warm against the side of her neck.

She settled against him. "Not anymore," she murmured, tracing the outline of his mouth with the tip of an index finger.

His teeth nipped at her finger lightly. "This is cozy. We're so well hidden, nobody could find us here."

"I feel as though the world is far away."

"Let's pretend we're on a desert island," he said quietly, and bent to kiss the corner of her mouth. "Just the two of us. There isn't another living soul for a thousand miles." He shifted until he was half reclining on the car seat, and turned her to lie atop him. "We've got all the time in the world."

"Yes." Samantha's lids lowered as she settled her head on his shoulder. "It's a lovely fantasy."

For a while she lost herself in the lovemaking. If only it were more than a fantasy, she thought dazedly. If only she didn't have to deal with the worrying differences between them. If only he'd been born of working-class parents instead of one of the Philadelphia Fitzgeralds.

"I forgot," she murmured, lifting her head to break the kiss. "I promised your grandmother I'd phone her and tell her what happened."

"You can phone her later," he muttered, pulling her back down for his kiss.

She shook off the pleasurable, melting warmth. "No, Tobin. We have to get to a telephone. She'll be walking the floor worrying."

He cursed softly and allowed her to extricate herself from his hold. "You're right," he grumbled. He shifted and started the engine. After backing the big car carefully into the road, he patted the seat beside him. She slid across and into the crook of his arm. "After we phone Grandmother, we'll go to my place. I can return her car tomorrow."

At the moment she wasn't in a mood to argue. "All right."

He turned his head and placed a kiss on her temple. "I've been thinking."

"What about?"

"If you're brave enough to face two criminals alone, you can surely face my family and friends at the symphony ball."

She leaned her head on his shoulder. "A sneaky line of reasoning if I ever heard one."

"You're not afraid of them, are you?" His tone held a mixture of amusement and challenge.

"Absolutely not!"

"Good. Then you'll allow me to escort you to the ball?"

Samantha sighed. He'd outmaneuvered her, and she'd let him. Well, what did it matter? Her going to the ball wouldn't solve any of their problems, but she couldn't imagine how it could make them worse. "All right, Tobin. I'll go."

Samantha knew almost immediately that it had been a mistake to come to the symphony ball with Tobin. She had used her credit card to buy an emerald silk gown that was much too expensive. It would take her six months to pay for it, but when she saw the glamorous designer originals most of the other women were wearing, she felt dowdy by comparison.

"I shouldn't have come," she said, after Tobin had led her away from yet another of his social acquaintances. This one, a sixtyish matron dripping diamonds, had remarked, "Preston, Preston . . . you must be one of the New York Prestons." Samantha had smiled noncommittally. Now she said, "I don't belong with these people, Tobin. Did you see how that woman was sizing me up? She knew I wasn't one of the New York Prestons."

Tobin tucked her hand under his arm. "You're the most beautiful woman here. That's why she was giving you the once-over. Envious, no doubt. Her own daughters are as ugly as posts."

She knew he was trying to cheer her up, but it didn't help.

"I just saw my parents come in," Tobin said. "I'll introduce you."

This was the moment Samantha had been dreading ever since she had agreed to come. Tobin had taken her hand and was making a path through the well-dressed crowd. He glanced over his shoulder and must have seen her reluctance in her face. "They don't bite, love."

She had no chance to reply. Tobin Grantham Fitzgerald II and his stately, dark-haired wife were watching them curiously. "Samantha," Tobin said, "I'd like you to meet my parents. Mother, Father, this is Samantha Preston."

"How do you do," Samantha murmured.

Tobin's father cleared his throat. "Well, well, this is a nice surprise. You're new to Philadelphia, Miss Preston, I take it. Or are you merely visiting?"

"No, I've lived here most of my life."

"Who are your parents?"

Tobin cut in smoothly. "Samantha's parents are dead."

"Forgive me, Miss Preston. That was a thoughtless question."

"It's all right," Samantha replied, warming to Tobin's father. "They've been gone a long time. My uncle Sam raised me." Touched by a sudden spurt of defiance she added, "I run the detective agency Uncle Sam left to me."

Tobin's mother, whose ice-blue eyes had been studying Samantha intently, blinked and sucked in her breath, as though somebody had thrown ice water in her face. She blinked again and partly recovered from the shock of learning Samantha's chosen occupation. "Tobin, I was under the impression you were coming to the ball with Dorothy Coulter."

That voice could cut steel, Samantha thought, feeling disapproval emanating from the woman in waves. The haughty Rose Fitzgerald, who had given Eleanor so much trouble.

"Obviously you've been laboring under a false impression, Mother," Tobin said.

Rose Fitzgerald's penetrating stare made Samantha want to shrivel up and disappear. She was beginning to feel a little sick. Fortunately, the orchestra struck up a tune at that moment.

"Dance with me, Samantha?" Tobin asked.

"Yes," Samantha answered gratefully as Tobin led her toward the dance floor. When they were out of earshot of Tobin's parents, Samantha whispered, "Who's Dorothy Coulter?"

"A woman I dated a few times over a year ago. We grew up together."

"Your mother thinks you're still seeing her."

"She knows better."

"She didn't appear to. You should keep her better informed, Tobin."

He laughed shortly. "Not necessary. She and her friends have a grapevine that won't quit."

She mentioned another woman to hurt me, Samantha mused. She was sure Rose Fitzgerald could be a formidable opponent.

"Damn," Tobin muttered under his breath. "Here comes Maida. Well, she was bound to track me down sooner or later." The woman hurrying toward them with a dazzling smile on her face was blond, elegant, and beautiful. *Exactly the sort of woman Tobin should be with instead of me,* Samantha told herself. The blonde rushed up to Tobin and kissed his cheek. "Where on earth have you been keeping yourself, darling? We haven't seen you in ages."

"Sorry I couldn't make it to your dinner party, Maida. Where's Richard?"

"He had a late board meeting. He'll be here soon." She glanced at Samantha, smiling expectantly.

Tobin took Samantha's hand, a gesture that wasn't lost on the beautiful blonde. "Samantha, this is Maida Nettleson. Maida, Samantha Preston."

"I'm Tobin's sister-in-law," Maida added, shaking Samantha's hand.

"My former sister-in-law," Tobin amended.

"Were you at Vassar or Smith?" Maida inquired.

"Neither," Samantha said.

Maida's brows arched in surprise. So, this was Charlotte Fitzgerald's sister. Tobin's wife must have been a beautiful blonde, too, like her sister. Feeling totally outclassed Samantha wished fervently that she were anyplace else in the world.

"Please excuse us, Maida," Tobin was saying. "I want to dance with Samantha."

Upon reaching the dance floor Samantha went into Tobin's arms as though he were a safe harbor in a storm. "Obviously, I'm a big shock to everybody," she said. "You've told them nothing about me."

"There's been no opportunity. Samantha?"

She looked up at him reluctantly.

"I'm very proud of you, sweetheart. If they're surprised, it's because they can't imagine what a beautiful woman like you sees in me."

"Oh, Tobin." She smiled softly as his arm tightened around her.

He bent his head to whisper in her ear. "For the sake of propriety we'll stay for a few dances. But I'm whisking you away from here as soon as I can. I want you to myself."

She drew away from him to see his face, and he lightly kissed her mouth. She held on to him, feeling dizzy. "Oh, Tobin, I want you," she breathed. The need was sudden, unexpected, and urgent.

His mouth touched hers again. She was only faintly aware of the heads that turned in their direction. "That," he said huskily, "can be arranged." He swung her around, making her gown swirl about her feet.

She gave a shaky laugh. "Do you think I'm a bold hussy?"

His hand ran down her side to her hip. "I think you're an enchantress."

Color stained her cheeks. Sighing, she nestled her head against his shoulder, their bodies swaying with the dreamy music. As long as she and Tobin were alone, she felt desirable, cherished, invulnerable. But he had a family and friends. No two people could live their lives separated from other people. She pushed her misgivings aside. With her eyes closed, and Tobin's arms around her, she could pretend there were no curious and disapproving eyes watching them. Until the music stopped . . .

CHAPTER TEN

Tobin left for Los Angeles on business the day after the symphony ball. The preceding night he had made love to Samantha with a tenderness that made her weep.

In the dreamy afterglow of loving, Tobin had asked, "Why are you crying, my darling?"

"Because I love you."

He had sheltered her securely in his strong arms and dried her tears with his fingers. "And I love you. Is that cause for tears?"

That evening at the ball she had decided that they must be honest with each other. They must face the painful truth now; the longer they denied it, the harder it would be to face. "Yes . . . oh, Tobin, love isn't enough. There are too many obstacles."

"My parents, you mean." He knew it would be useless to try to smooth over their reaction to Samantha at the ball. In time he thought his father would come to accept Samantha, but his mother probably never would. "Sweetheart, this is none of their business."

"You're not being realistic. Of course it's their

business. You're their only son." She couldn't be the cause of estrangement between Tobin and his parents. If that happened, Tobin might eventually come to resent her. She couldn't bear that.

"Then they'd damn well better show respect for the woman I love," he muttered.

Samantha wasn't naive enough to bank her future on things said while the sweet memory of their lovemaking was still so vivid. "You're a nice man, Tobin," she murmured.

His hand stroked her thigh, then cupped her hip to pull her hard against him. "We belong together, even if the whole world is against it." His mouth claimed hers in a kiss of possession. Finally he asked, "Don't you agree?"

"At the moment, yes." She gave a shaky laugh and searched for his lips again. "At the moment I can believe anything."

"I'm talking about more than the moment." His tongue penetrated the honeyed interior of her mouth. "You do understand that, don't you?"

"Just kiss me again," she murmured. "Kiss me and don't say anything else."

She wanted to relish every second of her time with Tobin. Tomorrow he would fly to Los Angeles for a week of business meetings. She wouldn't be able to taste him or touch him or feel his hands on her. He would have a full week to reconsider the impulsive promises made in the throes of passion. A week to think about the importance of approval from his family and friends. A week to have second thoughts about throwing away the standards ingrained over thirty-five years. The memory of their few weeks together would blur and change. How could she let him leave her tonight? How could she keep him with her? She would make these few hours so precious that the memory of them would last a lifetime.

"Tobin, love me . . . just love me."

When he left her at dawn, his last words were "Don't worry, love. We'll work it out."

The words were a tiny thread of hope in the following days, a thread that she clutched tightly. A thread that was strengthened by Tobin's nightly phone calls. "If we love each other," he told her over and over, "we can overcome any obstacle."

Samantha had just showered and dried her hair Wednesday night when her doorbell rang. She pulled on a terry robe, stepped into terry mules, and hurried to the front door. She turned on the porch light and, leaving the safety chain engaged, cracked the door. Beside her, Churchill growled low in his throat. She shushed him and peered through the crack. For an instant she was sure the woman was an illusion. What would Tobin's sister-in-law be doing in this neighborhood? The feeling of unreality passed and Samantha released the chain and opened the door wider. "Yes?"

"Miss Preston, I'm Maida Nettleson. We met at the symphony ball. Do you remember?"

"Of course. Come in, Mrs. Nettleson."

Maida swept a glance over the room, a glance that seemed to label everything tasteless and gauche. "I had a rather difficult time finding your address. I'm not familiar with this part of town."

No doubt, Samantha thought. Churchill sniffed

at Maida's Italian designer pumps and growled. "Come with me," Samantha ordered the dog. She put him in the kitchen and closed the door. Maida was still standing where she'd left her. "Won't you sit down," Samantha said. She waited until Maida had seated herself gingerly on the edge of the sofa, then settled into the rocker and resigned herself to what was sure to be an unpleasant conversation. It was obvious from the grim set of Maida's beautiful mouth that she hadn't come with pleasantries in mind.

Maida swept another look over the room's furnishings, and for a moment Samantha saw it all through Maida's eyes. Samantha had attempted to disguise the shabbiness with plants and bright colors. She saw now that her optimistic attempt had not really succeeded.

"Interesting," said Maida, and brought her gaze back to Samantha.

"I'm sure you didn't come here to get a look at my home. What can I do for you?"

Maida smoothed her navy-and-green silk skirt over her knees, then folded her hands in her lap. "Have you heard from Tobin since he arrived in L.A.?"

"I can't imagine why you'd be interested." *I will not let you intimidate me,* Samantha vowed silently. *I will not be flustered into saying things I'll regret.* "Why don't you just get to the point, Mrs. Nettleson?"

"I've done a little checking into your background, Samantha." Maida's clasped fingers tightened. It was the only outward sign that beneath the classically beautiful exterior ran strong emotion. "Apparently your uncle made a modest living as a private investigator, but since you took over, the agency has been on the brink of bankruptcy."

"You had somebody investigate me?" Samantha felt her temper flaring and tried to dampen it.

"One of your more prosperous peers." Maida unclasped her hands and spread them out above her knees, as though to admire them. She tapped a glossy fingernail on her right knee. "His report made intriguing reading. I was particularly interested in the fact that your aunt, Ruby Preston, holds a very low opinion of you. Since she raised you from the age of ten, I can only presume she knows you well and has good reason to dislike you."

"I have no intention of discussing my aunt with you." Samantha's voice was low and tightly controlled.

Maida's eyes widened; she had noticed the ruffling of Samantha's calm. It was probably the reaction she'd wanted. "I doubt that you could tell me much that I don't already know. Ruby Preston doesn't share your reticence. She talked quite freely with my investigator. It seems you finagled her out of her inheritance when your uncle died."

"Hardly. My uncle left the agency to me. Aunt Ruby received the insurance money, a great deal more than the value of the agency."

"She doesn't see it that way, I'm afraid."

"I don't really care how she sees it, Mrs. Nettleson. You've obviously done your homework. Are you trying to impress me?"

"I want you to understand that I'm an extremely determined woman."

"And not averse to sticking your nose in other people's business."

"Grant is my nephew. Whatever touches him is my business. Furthermore, the decision to hire an investigator was not mine alone. I conferred with Tobin's mother. Rose has seen the report and encouraged me to have this little talk with you. I speak for both of us. If you'd like to confirm that, I suggest you call Rose Fitzgerald right now."

"I think not. I must ask you again to get to the point."

"Very well. Your existence can fairly be described as hand to mouth, and your future prospects are no better, since your business is failing. I understand how you could be attracted to the idea of improving your situation."

"What are you suggesting?" Samantha felt angry tremors in the pit of her stomach.

"Do I really have to spell it out for you?" Maida folded her hands again. "Tobin is an extremely wealthy man, and he's been a widower for four years now. You might say he's ripe for the picking. You're an attractive woman, Samantha, I don't deny that. Unfortunately you've come into Tobin's life at the worst possible time. Lonely men make unwise decisions when under the spell of a pretty woman."

"So you and Tobin's mother have taken it upon yourselves to make those decisions for him, is that right?" Samantha fought to keep her voice steady. "After meeting me briefly once, you've concluded I'm a fortune hunter." She gave Maida a long, level look. "You've got a colossal nerve, lady. Have you ever thought that I might care for Tobin?"

"I'm sure you've convinced Tobin that you do." Maida studied Samantha in silence for a long moment, as though giving Samantha time to digest her last words. "You aren't the first woman of your type to try to take my sister's place. I doubt that you'll be the last." She gave a careless shrug. "And you're the least likely of the lot to succeed. Tobin has no intention of marrying you, you know."

Samantha gripped the arms of the rocker to keep from jumping to her feet and ordering the woman out of the house. She sat very still, tight with control. "Then you've wasted your time coming here, haven't you?"

"Rose and I thought you needed to be reminded of the realities of your situation. You obviously don't belong in Tobin's world and you never will. After the symphony ball, even you should be able to see that. There is no substitute for breeding, the right background, the right schools." Maida threw another contemptuous glance around the room. "I'm not saying it's fair, Samantha. It's simply true. No matter how much you might want to fit in, you will never be able to bring it off. Tobin may be infatuated now and think he doesn't care, but there will come a time when he will. He'll be embarrassed by your lack of education and social skills. He'll resent being excluded from the activities of lifelong friends. And he would be excluded,

Samantha. You will never be accepted in Tobin's circle."

Maida's words sent a thrill of fear through Samantha, because the woman was saying things she'd told herself in the few, brief, honest moments she'd allowed herself since meeting Tobin. "I don't care to hear any more of this." She came to her feet.

Maida stood, too, and faced Samantha. "If you really love Tobin, you'll let him go. It's the kindest, most loving thing you can do for him—and for Grant."

Samantha's fear increased. "Tobin will have something to say about that."

Maida tossed her head elegantly. "Not if you go where he can't find you."

"That's an outrageous suggestion. This is my home."

"If you don't get out of Tobin's life—all the way out—Rose has instructed me to inform you that she will sue him for Grant's custody."

"That's ridiculous." Samantha suddenly felt cold, her skin clammy. "She wouldn't have a chance in hell of succeeding."

"That may be." Maida moved slowly past Samantha to the door. What would it take to disturb the woman's self-confidence? "But she could keep it in the courts for years. Think how unpleasant that would be for Tobin and Grant."

"She wouldn't do that to her own son and grandson." Samantha's unsteady words sounded more like a plea than a statement.

"She would, if she thought it would be better for them in the long run."

The chill had crept inside Samantha now. She shivered. "What kind of woman would put them through such an ordeal, just to get her own way?"

"I am merely passing along the message." Maida took a breath and opened the door. "You can prevent it happening. Only you. Do we understand each other?"

"Perfectly," Samantha agreed. Her throat was so constricted that she could barely push the word out. She struggled to keep tears from filling her eyes.

"I told Rose you'd be reasonable. If you will get in touch with me when you've relocated, I'll see that you have enough money to get started in another business."

"Get out," Samantha whispered. "My love doesn't have a price tag on it. Whatever I decide, it will be what I think is best for Tobin and Grant. But you wouldn't know about unselfish decisions, Mrs. Nettleson." She managed to hold her tears in until the woman was gone.

Samantha put Churchill in the backyard and made it upstairs to her bedroom before sobs racked her.

When she'd cried herself dry, she roamed the dark house. Tobin wouldn't be back in town for another four days; thank goodness she had time to pull herself together and decide what to do. *Let me make the right decision for Tobin and Grant*, she prayed, as she moved down the stairs and

160

through the shadowed living room like someone in a dream.

By dawn she knew what she had to do. She'd been blind to reality, blinded by her love for Tobin. In the beginning she'd known that a relationship with Tobin could only end by hurting her. Love had made her close her eyes to what she wanted desperately not to see; but it was because she loved him that she had to let him go. Once the decision was made, a merciful numbness came over her.

When she walked into the agency office the next morning, Billy Bob's first words were "What's wrong?" His eyes narrowed in concern as he studied her. "You look like the very devil."

"Billy Bob, you know I've been worried for months about our financial situation." She saw his concerned look deepen and patted his shoulder fondly. "I've tried to keep current on our expenses, but all I've done is fall farther behind."

"Samantha." He unfolded his skinny length from his steno chair in alarm. "You're not giving up, are you?"

"It's time, Billy Bob. I'm going to put the agency on the market for whatever it will bring. Maybe the new owner will keep you on. If not, I know you'll have no trouble finding another job."

"I don't want another job, Samantha. And I don't want to stay here and work for somebody else."

"Billy Bob, try to put yourself in my place." If he continued to oppose her, she'd end in tears. After last night she'd thought there could be no more tears in her. Yet already she felt the hot sting of threatened moisture in her eyes. "Nobody can keep going in the hole, month after month, regardless of how much he likes what he's doing. There comes a point when you have to admit defeat and regroup. You're a good employee and a loyal friend, but I have to sell the agency."

"What will you do then?" He sounded like a child who'd just had a dream smashed.

"I'm going to start over somewhere else. In fact, I probably won't be in the office after today. I can give you six weeks' salary as severance pay. I wish it could be more, but it should be enough to carry you until you find another job."

He was staring at her incredulously. "You're leaving Philadelphia? Maybe it's none of my business, Samantha, but it sounds to me like you're throwing out the baby with the bath water."

She managed a smile. "I know it does, but this isn't a decision I made lightly. I have to leave Philadelphia. I can't explain why."

"Where will you go?"

"I've always thought I'd like to move South—Florida, maybe," she replied vaguely. She hugged him tightly, then drew back. "I'm going to miss you, pal."

"I'm gonna miss you too." His voice cracked.

"I may have to entrust some information to you before I leave." She hesitated, then shook her head. "We'll talk about that later."

"You can depend on me to keep your secrets."

"I know I can." She went to her desk, picked up the phone book, and turned to the section titled

Real Estate Agents. "By the way, Billy Bob, would you like to have Delilah?"

"Your white Persian? Sure. Are you planning to give away all your pets?"

"I'll take Churchill with me. He's too old to adjust to somebody else. But I'll have to find homes for the cats. If you'll take Delilah, I think I can get people in my neighborhood to take the other two."

"You're really burning your bridges. Are you going to sell your house too?"

Oddly, the idea of relinquishing her home was even harder to accept than giving up the agency. "I don't know. Maybe I'll rent it for a while." The monthly income would be a godsend while she settled somewhere and found a job.

"Samantha?"

The forlorn note in his voice made her hand stop midway to the telephone. She turned to look at him. "What?"

"Will you write and let me know how you're getting along?"

"You bet." She turned away quickly, to hide her tear-filled eyes from him. She cleared her throat and reached for the phone.

By Friday she had listed the agency for sale and the house for lease with the same real estate concern. She had found homes for the three cats, sold most of her furniture, and stored the few pieces she couldn't bear to part with. Her car was serviced and ready to go; she would leave early Saturday morning. She'd confided to Billy Bob that there was someone whom she didn't want to find her and promised to write him after she was settled. She didn't tell him that she wouldn't send him her address, so there would be no way for him to reply. Perhaps she was being overcautious, but she knew Billy Bob would be no match for Tobin, if Tobin decided to extract information from him.

The only thing left was to manage somehow to talk to Tobin when he phoned Friday night, without his getting an inkling of what she was up to. It was the most difficult thing she'd ever done.

When she heard his voice, memories rushed in on her, almost overwhelming her. *If only I could have one last night with him*, she thought. *What will he think when he comes back and finds I've gone? Will he hurt as much as I'm hurting?* One thing she knew, he wouldn't understand. But after he got over the shock, maybe he'd be relieved. She braced herself. Such thoughts would only make the pain more intense. It was over.

"Hello, Tobin."

"Samantha, you sound odd. Are you all right?"

"I'm perfectly fine, just a little tired from cleaning house." *And packing and preparing to leave you. Oh, Tobin, how can I live without you?*

"This week has seemed like a year. I miss you."

"I miss you too." *I will always miss you, my darling.*

"You've changed my life, Samantha. I can't think how I survived before I found you."

Her fingers gripped the receiver so hard, there was no feeling in them. His words were drowning her in pain. Rose Fitzgerald's threat gave her the strength to keep up the charade a few minutes more. "You've changed my life too. I'll never regret having met you."

"*Regret.* That's a strange word to use. I've no intention of letting you regret it. Are you sure you're all right, sweetheart?"

Her hand gripping the receiver was beginning to shake. She clasped it with her other hand to keep it still. She had to stay calm. Only a few minutes more.

"Yes, I'm all right. Tobin . . ."

"Yes, love?"

"I"—she wanted to say that she loved him, one last time. But that wouldn't be fair—"I was wondering when you're coming home." Her voice was tight with grief.

"Tomorrow evening. My plane lands there at seven-thirty. Do you think you can meet me? I'm starving for the sight of you."

"I'll try." It was a necessary lie.

"Try hard, love. I want to touch you and hold you, Samantha. I need you more than I've ever needed anyone."

Nausea was rising to her throat. She was beginning to tremble all over now. She wished he'd hang up and bring an end to this torture. "I know," she whispered. "I know because I'd give everything I have if you could be here with me right now."

"I'll be there tomorrow night. Just twenty-four hours. Do you think we can survive until then?"

Samantha closed her eyes a moment. "We can survive whatever we have to survive. People are stronger than they know." She had to believe that was true.

"You're very pensive this evening."

Her head was beginning to throb. She swallowed. "I have these moods."

"I'm learning new things about you all the time."

She managed a shaky imitation of a laugh. "You may decide I'm too much trouble."

"Not a chance. I love you, Samantha."

I love you too. Desperately. But she couldn't say the words. The memory of Tobin's kiss, his hands on her skin, made her nearly senseless with sorrow. *What am I doing to you?* The image of Maida's cool, determined face floated before her. People did what they had to do. "Thank you for that, Tobin." Her voice was low and steady with resignation. She had stopped hoping for a miracle. She had stopped struggling against the inevitable. "I have to go now. I'm so tired I'm about to faint."

"All right. Get a good night's rest. See you tomorrow."

"Good-bye, Tobin."

Nothing was forever. In time she would be able to think of him without wanting to die. In time he'd realize she'd done what was best. In time he might even forgive her.

CHAPTER ELEVEN

Samantha stopped on the sidewalk in front of the bookshop. She'd noticed the sign in the window yesterday during her morning walk. It was still there this morning. She read it again. FULL-TIME SALESPERSON WANTED. OPPORTUNITY FOR ADVANCEMENT. INQUIRE WITHIN.

Since arriving in Key West a month ago, she'd rented a small house on the beach and moved in. Daily walks had familiarized her with the small-town resort community. She had been looking for a job for two weeks and was dismayed by the dismal prospects for somebody with her qualifications—or lack of them. Working in a bookstore sounded more interesting than the other available jobs.

As she entered, the bell on the door jangled. It was a small shop with shelves built to fit every available space. She saw no one; whoever was running the place was evidently in a back room. While she waited, she browsed among the book-crammed shelves. The shop's stock was surprisingly varied. There was one section, near the door, devoted to the works of Hemingway, who, before

167

his death, had been the Key's most famous resident, and books about every conceivable aspect of Key West's history and culture.

"May I help you?"

She turned to see a tall, gray-haired woman, wearing a green bibbed apron over a cotton shirtwaist dress.

Samantha smiled. "I hope so. I'm Samantha Preston. I've come about the job."

The woman untied the apron and tossed it over a rattan chair that stood with its twin in a cozy reading corner. She tucked a falling strand of gray hair into the bun on the back of her head. "You'll have to forgive the way I look. I've been cleaning up in back. I'm expecting a load of new books any day." She glanced about the shop and sighed. "Though heaven knows where I'll put them." She waved a hand toward the door at the back leading from the shop area. "If I can get rid of some of the junk my late husband accumulated, I'll have more shelves built in back."

"What sort of junk?"

"Old *National Geographics,* stacks of out-of-date Florida history texts, that sort of thing. My husband could never bring himself to part with anything printed."

Samantha laughed. "I know what you mean. It's difficult for me to throw away a magazine or book, no matter how dog eared. When I packed to move to Key West, I had boxes of them to dispose of. I finally called a used-book dealer, and he bought the lot. I couldn't bear to watch him cart them off, though."

"Ah." A pensive look came into the woman's eyes. "You'd have hit it off with Wiley."

"How long has it been since you lost your husband?"

"Almost three years." She smiled. "And I'm just now getting around to sorting through his things. Well"—she indicated one of the rattan chairs—"sit down and I'll put the fire on under the kettle. My name's Thelma Richards, by the way. Make yourself comfortable and I'll be back in a jiffy with some tea." She disappeared into the back room again.

Thelma returned within minutes with two mugs of hot tea. After waiting on a couple of customers she settled into the second rattan chair. "So, tell me something about yourself, Samantha. Have you worked in a bookstore before?"

"No. I had my own business until a month ago. I ran a detective agency in Pennsylvania. Business wasn't so good, so I decided to try something else." Samantha hesitated before she added, "Mrs. Richards, I love books, if that's any recommendation."

"Call me Thelma. And, yes, it's an essential quality in a bookseller. You'd never stick with it otherwise." Thelma studied Samantha Preston's face with a mixture of curiosity and hope. She'd interviewed five or six people for the job already, but she'd not been impressed by any of them. This young woman was, in fact, the first applicant who struck Thelma as both practical and intelligent; and she was rarely wrong with first impressions. Something was not quite right, though. There was a lingering aura of sadness about Samantha Preston. Perhaps it had something to do with the cause of her relocation from Pennsylvania to Florida. "Where are you living?"

"A rented beach cottage about a mile north of here. I could walk to work, which may be necessary. My car's mileage indicator rolled past a hundred thousand on the drive down."

"Everybody walks in Key West." Thelma sipped her tea. "Any family back in Pennsylvania?"

"No."

She obviously didn't want to talk about that. "You'd have to work odd hours. I stay open until eight three evenings a week, and during the tourist season the shop is open seven days."

"The hours would be no problem. There's nobody waiting for me at the cottage but my dog."

There was more behind that remark than met the eye, Thelma would wager. "If we suit each other, I'd want to train you to manage the shop. I'd like to spend some time up north with my daughters. I could only pay minimum wage the first two months, until we see how it goes."

Samantha quickly calculated how much was left in her checking account. Barely enough to supplement her wages for two months. But if the agency could be sold during that time, there would be more. Anyway, she wasn't exactly in a position to haggle. "That sounds satisfactory."

"When could you start?"

Samantha set her mug on the floor beside her chair. "Anytime, but before you decide, there's something you should know." Her eyes darkened and she drew in her breath. "I'm pregnant."

"Oh." Thelma bent her head over her cup; it gave her time to decide what to say next. "Are you widowed or divorced?" It would explain the suggestion of sadness in Samantha's eyes.

"I've never been married."

"I see." Thelma wasn't as shocked as she once would have been. Single mothers weren't all that uncommon these days. "When is your baby due?"

"February. The doctor says I'm very healthy. I'd want to work right up until delivery, and I'll need to come back to work as soon as I can make satisfactory arrangements for the baby." She'd been in Key West less than three weeks when she'd gone in for a pregnancy test and confirmed her growing suspicion that she was carrying Tobin's child. After the shock had worn off, she had found that the idea of the baby wasn't altogether unpleasant. There would be problems, of course, but nothing she couldn't cope with. And already she loved this child.

"Obviously you've decided to keep the baby."

"Oh, yes." Samantha laced her fingers together. "If you'd rather not have a pregnant saleslady around, I'll understand."

Thelma liked this young woman. Apparently she had given little thought to terminating her pregnancy. Nor had she considered putting it up for adoption. She accepted her responsibilities, and Thelma admired that. Observing the nervous movement of Samantha's hands Thelma gave her a direct look. "What I want is somebody I can depend on to be here when she's expected and do what she's supposed to do. Whether or not she's pregnant is beside the point."

"I'll be very dependable."

"I believe you will be." Thelma smiled and extended her hand. "Shall we say nine o'clock tomorrow morning?"

"Nine o'clock's fine. Thank you." Samantha shook the proffered hand, then smiled. "You won't be sorry."

Thelma lifted her brows. "I don't expect to be."

Tobin was back in the office full time now, after a month of running around Philadelphia like a wild man, searching for clues to Samantha's whereabouts. He'd badgered the real estate agent who had contracted to sell Samantha's business until the woman refused to return his calls. He'd talked to the people who had rented Samantha's house and had gone from door to door in the neighborhood, asking questions. He had even tracked down Samantha's former secretary, Billy Bob Digby, who was now training to become a court stenographer. All he had learned was that Samantha had mentioned something about moving to a warm climate, possibly Florida. He had spent one ten-hour day with a map of Florida before him, calling information operators in every Florida town of any size and asking for Samantha Preston's number. It had eventually occurred to him that, since she obviously didn't want to be found, she'd have asked for an unlisted number.

The madness had passed when he could no longer think of anything else to do to find Samantha. She had left him. It had taken a month, but he'd finally managed to accept it. She didn't want to see him. He had no clear idea why. But had he ever really understood Samantha? One morning he woke up and looked at his gaunt, beard-stubbled face in the mirror, and knew he had to go on with his life or go truly crazy. He had to forget her.

At the end of his third day back at work his father requested a late-afternoon meeting with Tobin in his office. When Tobin arrived, his father mixed bourbon-and-waters for both of them. "Glad you decided to return to the firm, Tobin. Your mother and I have been very worried about you."

Tobin lounged in a deep leather chair and took a swallow of his drink. "I'm all right."

His father sat facing Tobin. His expression was drawn with concern. "If you don't mind my saying so, you don't look all right. I take it you've found no trace of Samantha Preston."

Tobin looked up in surprise. It was out of character for his father to talk to him about personal things. Their relationship had always been distanced. He hadn't mentioned Samantha to his father since he'd returned from L.A. and learned she was gone. A month ago he'd told his father merely that he needed some time off. It startled Tobin to realize that his father had known all along what he was doing. He made a futile gesture with his glass. "No. People who are determined not to be found usually succeed. I'm coming to grips with that."

His father's blue eyes assessed him shrewdly.

"You're very much in love with this young woman."

Tobin made a sound of self-contempt. "Considering how I've been behaving lately, that must be obvious to everyone."

"Your mother thought it was merely a passing fancy, that it would blow over."

Tobin's lips curled into the semblance of a smile. "Mother thinks what it pleases her to think. You know that."

"Yes . . . hmmm." He comtemplated the contents of his glass reflectively.

"One positive thing has come out of this," Tobin commented. "I now understand how Grandfather felt about Grandmother and how easy it must have been to defy convention and marry her. I used to think of what he did as very courageous. But it wasn't. It was simply what he had to do. It's easy when you love someone." In a rare moment of confidence Tobin added quietly, "I've never loved anyone as I love Samantha, Dad, not even Charlotte. When I let myself think about it, my future looks bleak without her."

"Then you must keep looking for her."

His father continued to surprise Tobin. "Don't let Mother hear you say that."

"This is between you and Samantha. Your mother has nothing to do with it."

Tobin had always known that, but he hadn't been sure his father had. He hesitated, then confided, "I've been thinking about hiring a private investigator. I don't know where he could look for clues that I haven't, but at least I'd feel I'm doing something." He had to know why she had run away. Perhaps if he could find her, talk to her, he'd be able to understand and let her go. He finished his drink and rose.

His father cleared his throat. "There's no need to mention this little talk to your mother, of course."

Tobin smiled dryly. "Of course."

He went back to his office and looked at the telephone number he'd written on a notepad his first day back at work. It was the number of a highly recommended private detective. Perhaps he'd put off calling because this was his last resort. If the detective couldn't find Samantha, there wouldn't even be the tiny sliver of hope that now remained to Tobin.

Taking a deep breath he lifted the receiver and dialed the number.

It was October almost before Samantha realized it. Tourists still streamed to Key West, though not as many as during the summer. Not that the weather on the Key had changed all that much; it was still warm and sunny. The halycon days could continue, natives told her, until Christmas. And winter would be nothing like the winters back home. "Pay attention, Samantha," one customer of the bookshop had joked, "or you'll miss winter altogether."

In Philadelphia the leaves would be turning to brilliant golds and oranges and reds, the days would be invigoratingly crisp, the nights cold enough for a blanket. Samantha missed the changing seasons; continuous summer could get monotonous.

The baby was beginning to show a bit now, though loose garments still disguised her condition to all but the most astute. Those who noticed that she was pregnant were usually mothers. "I'd recognize that look anywhere," one of them told Samantha. "Your breasts are fuller, and there's a glow to your skin. I've had five kids—I should know."

Recently she'd felt the baby move, a little flutter of feeling. It happened mostly at night and occasionally woke her. She would lie in bed as she was doing now, and imagine what the baby would look like. She knew there was a test available that would tell her the baby's sex, but she didn't take it. She didn't really care which it was. All she wanted was a healthy child, and she felt assured of that. A sickly baby couldn't be as active as this one.

The agency had been sold. She'd signed the final papers two weeks ago and returned them to the real estate company. She had used some of the proceeds to turn the cottage's spare bedroom into a yellow-and-white nursery. The balance was tucked away in a money market account—her emergency fund. Security was something she hadn't thought much about before, but with the baby coming her outlook was changing. She had decided to sell the house in Philadelphia, too, and add the money to her savings. The decision to sell the house had been a wrenching one, because it was her last tie with Philadelphia. Selling it was more than giving up the house; it was giving up the past.

And Tobin. She turned on her side, seeking a more comfortable position. The baby kicked in protest, and Samantha placed her hand on her stomach, smiling in the darkness. As long as she had Tobin's baby, she would never have to give him up completely. The baby would probably have his brown eyes, and every time she looked at those eyes, she'd think of Tobin.

She reached for the spare pillow and hugged it against her tender breasts. The real estate agent had told her that Tobin had made repeated requests at his office for Samantha's new address. Following Samantha's wishes they had refused the information. Tobin must have given up trying to find her by now. Was he seeing somebody else? Had he forgotten her?

Had he improved his relationship with Grant? She hoped so. She would have enjoyed being around to watch Grant grow into the man she imagined he would be.

The little fluttery kicks continued. *This kid is going to be a gymnast,* Samantha mused. She rolled on her back again, but sleep was far away. It must be nearly dawn. She pulled herself from the bed and padded barefoot to the kitchen. She switched on a light and peered at the wall clock. Four thirty-five. She made coffee and sat at the kitchen table, where an open window admitted the cool gulf breeze. She sipped the coffee slowly, savoring the first of the two daily cups of decaffeinated she allowed herself during her pregnancy.

Churchill had followed her to the kitchen and draped himself across her bare feet. "You're a spoiled brat," Samantha told him, and he whined, as though in agreement. "You'd better enjoy it while you can. When the baby comes, I'll be too busy to pamper you."

She sat gazing out the window until a golden glow appeared on the horizon, announcing the coming of dawn. "I'll take good care of you, baby," Samantha whispered. "I'm sorry you'll never know your father, but I'll love you enough for both of us."

Thelma watched Samantha arranging travel books on the new shelves she had added to the back room. "I'll get the top shelves," she cautioned. "Don't you try anything dumb like climbing on a chair."

"Yes, Mother," Samantha returned, grinning at Thelma over her shoulder. She'd worked at the bookshop for three months now. It had turned out better than either she or Thelma could have hoped. They had become friends as well as business associates, and Samantha's salary now covered her basic living expenses. She enjoyed the work, though occasionally she suffered a pang when she thought about leaving the baby with a sitter while she came to the shop. Evidently Thelma was having the same misgivings. Recently she'd said, "When the baby comes, we could make room in the back for a crib, Samantha. Business will be slow until next spring. Between the two of us we should have time to care for the baby at least until then."

Samantha was considering Thelma's suggestion. By late spring the baby would be nearly four months old and she wouldn't worry quite as much about trusting him to a sitter.

The bell at the shop entrance jangled and Thelma went to the front to wait on the customer. Samantha reached for a memo pad and noted down areas of the country where their travel section was thin or nonexistent. She was hardly aware of the murmur of the male voice in the next room. She didn't even look around when she heard the sound of approaching footsteps.

"Another browser?" she asked musingly as she wrote *Montana* and *Idaho* on her pad. "We've had more of them this week, haven't we? They're probably making out their Christmas lists. I've seen several people looking through that country inns book. We'd better order another dozen and—"

Thelma's lack of response finally registered. Samantha glanced up and was paralyzed by shock.

Tobin watched her reach for the back of a chair for support. He saw the stunned widening of her eyes and the flicker of panic. It reminded him of a small, defenseless animal who realizes he's in a corner with no way out. She was afraid of him, and the knowledge made his stomach clench. The notepad slipped from her hands and landed on the floor at her feet. Her hands shook.

No, oh no, Samantha thought desperately, *don't*

let this be happening. I want to run, but I seem to have lost the use of my legs.

He watched her hands grip the chair back until the knuckles were white. The blood had drained from her face, leaving it ashen, but there was a soft luminescence shining through. She wore a loose dress with no waistline; it hid the feminine curves he remembered. But he hadn't remembered that she was so very beautiful. His eyes couldn't drink in enough of her, and he had to stuff his hands into his trouser pockets to keep them from reaching out to touch her. It seemed like a dozen lifetimes since he'd last seen her, not only four months. He remembered how her eyes had gone all soft and liquid when he made love to her. Her eyes weren't soft now, they were alert with watchfulness. How could she be afraid of him? On the flight down he'd told himself over and over that if she could look him in the face and say she didn't love him anymore, he would let her go, cut her out of his life forever. Now he knew he'd been lying to himself. He had to make her love him again. He couldn't go on living without her.

Samantha forced her fingers to release their grip on the chair. She straightened and braced herself with her back against the bookshelves. She willed her voice to be steady.

"You're a long way from home, Tobin."

Her voice, so cool and casual, was like a nail hammered into his heart. "I thought I'd never find you. If you hadn't sold the agency, I wouldn't have. The investigator I hired found the notice of the newly recorded deed. He was able to trace your address from that. I—I had to see you again, Samantha."

"Oh." Samantha forced her gaze to remain in the grip of his. "Well, here I am. As you can see, I'm well and perfectly content. So you can go back to Philadelphia with a clear conscience."

"For God's sake, will you shut up!" His voice was loud enough to be heard for a block. The months of anger and frustration and worry rushed out with the words, shaking him to the soles of his feet. "I'm not going anywhere until you tell me why you ran out on me without a word of explanation. You owe me that, Samantha. My life hasn't been worth dirt since you left!" He took a step toward her. "Dammit, Samantha . . ."

With a sudden, frightened movement she darted past him. "Keep your voice down! This is a business establishment. Please go, Tobin."

He looked as stricken as if she'd kicked him. "No." His voice wavered as he looked at her. "Not until we talk."

She stared at him. "We can't talk here." She didn't move for a moment, then she turned abruptly and walked into the front of the shop. Thelma was waiting on a woman customer. Both women looked at Samantha with intense curiosity. "Thelma, I need to leave for a little while. Can you manage until I get back?"

"Sure." Thelma's eyes were understanding. "Take all the time you need."

Tobin had appeared in the door to the back room, and Samantha said curtly, "We'll go for a walk." She practically ran to the door, not waiting for him to respond.

He caught up with her halfway down the block. She was walking with determined purpose toward the beach. He fell into step beside her, wanting to take her arm but afraid of what her reaction would be.

"Samantha—"

"Wait until we've reached my house," she said shortly. "It's not far from here." She didn't know if she could keep from crying, and she didn't want any more curious stares directed at them.

Somehow he managed not to speak again or touch her until they had entered a small frame cottage. Samantha had filled it with bright colors and green plants, like the house in Philadelphia. As soon as they were inside, she whirled to face him.

"Now, say what you have to say so I can get back to work."

The angry accusations that had been pushing at his lips drained out of him as he looked into her white face. "Oh, my God, Samantha . . ." It only required two steps to reach her and he pulled her against him so quickly she didn't have time to back away. He pressed her rigid body tightly against his, and for a long moment he couldn't speak. When he could, he asked thickly, "Why did you leave me?"

She felt her body relaxing against his, in spite of her efforts to resist. "It was the best way," she whispered. "A clean break, Tobin."

He looked down into her eyes. "I don't understand. . . ." His voice trailed off as he saw the fear jump back into her eyes. "In God's name, Samantha, why?"

She swallowed convulsively and shook her head, unable to reply.

He fought with himself for control and lost. Clasping her head in his hands he brought his mouth down on hers. The kiss was savage, hurting, an expression of his desperation. When he felt her resistance weakening, felt her body pressing against his, felt her mouth soften and open for him, he almost sobbed with relief. His hands ran over her, seeking her breasts beneath that damned voluminous dress. He clasped the full globes of her breasts, then with a moan, ran one hand down over her stomach. He was almost beyond reason, beyond hearing, when he realized that she was struggling to free herself.

"Tobin, no!" She was pushing his hand away from her stomach frantically. Her stomach . . .

His head came up and slowly his glazed eyes cleared. "Samantha?" He stared at her. "Oh, God, you're pregnant."

His arms loosened and she stepped back. She bowed her head for a moment, trying to compose herself. Then she looked at him. "It's all right, Tobin. I have it all figured out. I can take care of my baby."

He went on staring at her as if she were a stranger, a particularly monstrous stranger. "Our baby. You're carrying *our* baby. When did you intend to tell me, after the baby was born? No. You never meant to tell me at all, did you?"

"I—I thought it was best."

"You thought—!" He ran both hands through his hair and shook his head as if to clear it. "How could you think that?" he demanded furiously. She shrugged and turned her back. He wanted to grab her and shake her, force her to look at him. He wanted to yell and curse. He wanted to cry. He'd considered many reasons why she might have left him, but he'd never thought of this. She couldn't have believed he wouldn't want the child. She couldn't. . . . Several moments passed before he trusted himself to speak again.

"I don't care why you left me, Samantha," he said quietly. "That doesn't matter now. You have to come back, marry me, let me take care of you and the baby." If he could persuade her to come back, he'd have time to show her how much he loved her. Time to make her fall in love with him again.

"No, Tobin." Her voice was calm with the determination of a decision long made. "I can't."

He could no longer bear looking at her rigid back. He gripped her shoulders and turned her to face him. He would beg if he had to. "Please, Samantha. I love you."

He had thought her calm and detached. He was unprepared for the tears that filled her eyes and the desperation in her voice. "It's not enough!" She wrenched herself from his grasp.

"Tell me why," he pleaded. Unable to restrain himself he reached for her again. "Please, just tell me why."

She choked back a sob and walked away from

him. She stood, head bowed. "All right, Tobin, I'll tell you. While you were in Los Angeles, your sister-in-law came to see me."

"Maida?"

"Yes. She said things I'd known all along but had refused to face."

His expression was incredulous. "Such as?"

"That I could never fit into your world. I'd never be accepted by your family and friends. I—"

"Dear God, Samantha, do you think I care about that? I want you to be my wife. I don't care if the whole world hates it."

"There's more involved than what you and I want. We have to think about Grant."

What you and I want. The words caused a flame of hope to leap inside him. Did she mean that she wanted to marry him as much as he wanted it? Dear Lord, if that were only true. They could overcome anything if she still wanted him. "I've already talked to Grant. I told him if I could find you I was going to ask you to marry me. He's all for it, Samantha. He needs you, don't you know that? We both need you."

She wiped the tears from her cheeks with the back of her hand. "There's more. Maida spoke to your mother before she came to see me. Your mother threatened to sue you for Grant's custody if I didn't leave town. I couldn't stay and let Grant be torn between his father and his grandparents. I couldn't. . . ." Her voice was calm again, a dead sort of calm.

He crossed the room and touched her hair

gently. "I don't believe Mother said that. Maida was lying."

"But"—she took a deep breath—"I couldn't take the chance. What if she was telling the truth? Why would she lie?"

Carefully, he put his arm around her, and she let him. Gently, he led her to the couch. "Sit down and listen to me." She obeyed, like a robot, as if she had no will of her own. He sat beside her and took her hand; it lay cold and lifeless in his. "Maida has never forgiven me for marrying her sister. I was dating Maida when Charlotte and I started seeing each other. Maida had assumed we'd be married. When Charlotte died, she came to me and said she still loved me. She offered to get a divorce if I'd marry her. I was stunned. I'd had no idea that she still cared for me. I didn't handle it very well. I was still trying to pick up the pieces and decide how I was going to raise my son alone. I told her to get out of my house and never to come there alone again. What she said to you, sweetheart—it was Maida's way of getting revenge."

"Why would she say that about your mother when it would be so easy to find out if it were true?"

"Samantha, darling, I don't know." He hesitated. He'd memorized such grand things to say to her. Now that she sat beside him, carrying his child in her body, he couldn't remember any of the speeches he'd planned. "But it doesn't matter. Mother may have made a threat in anger, but she'd never go through with it. She's self-centered and used to having her own way, but she loves Grant. She wouldn't deliberately hurt him."

Samantha put her head back against the couch and closed her eyes. It was all too much for her. Maida had sounded as though she were telling the truth. What if Tobin was wrong about his mother? "She would never accept me."

"She'll accept you. I'll see to that. If she doesn't, she won't see me or her grandson again."

Her eyes flew open. "No, Tobin, I would hate myself if I were responsible for separating you from your parents."

"Dad knows why I'm here, and he completely approves. The last thing he said to me before I left was 'Son, turn the world upside down if you have to, but find that woman. You're not worth a damn without her.'"

She lifted her head. "He did?"

"Yes."

She took a deep breath. "Maida said if I really loved you, I'd leave you. I couldn't think about my own happiness. I had to think of you and Grant."

The ice that surrounded his heart was breaking up. She'd as much as said she still loved him. He wanted to say everything she needed to hear now. "Samantha, Maida's a shrewd judge of character. She knew you'd never put yourself ahead of those you loved."

"Tobin—"

"No, let me finish. I love you desperately. I'm willing to do anything if you'll marry me. We don't have to live in Philadelphia. We can live here, if you want. Or anywhere. None of that matters to me if we can be together." Slowly he brought his hand up to cup her cheek.

In his eyes Samantha saw swimming emotion and eloquent pleading. How could she send him away? Marriage would require major adjustments for both of them, but it was worth the risk to be with the man she loved and the father of her child. She leaned toward him. "I love you, Tobin."

He crushed her against him and, framing her face with his hands, kissed her deeply. Moments later he lifted his head. His eyes were intense as he said, "We'll get married here. We'll take all the time we need to decide where we want to live. Oh, my love, I thought I'd lost you for good." He claimed her mouth again in another tender yet passionate kiss.

Samantha wound her arms around his neck and moved into the sheltering strength of his arms. She and her baby were safe and protected there. Maybe, she thought as her heart soared, fairy tales could come true, after all.

Catch up with any Candlelights you're missing.

Here are the Ecstasies published this past June

ECSTASY SUPREMES $2.75 each

- [ ] 125 MOONLIGHT AND MAGIC, Melanie Catley.....15822-2-96
- [ ] 126 A LOVE TO LAST FOREVER,
      Linda Randall Wisdom......................15025-6-26
- [ ] 127 HANDFUL OF DREAMS, Heather Graham.....13420-X-30
- [ ] 128 THIS NIGHT AND ALWAYS, Kit Daley........16402-8-19

ECSTASY ROMANCES $2.25 each

- [ ] 434 DARE TO LOVE AGAIN, Rose Marie Ferris.....11698-8-21
- [ ] 435 THE THRILL OF HIS KISS, Marilyn Cunningham 18676-5-14
- [ ] 436 DAYS OF DESIRE, Saranne Dawson..........11712-7-15
- [ ] 437 ESCAPE TO PARADISE, Jo Calloway.........12365-8-47
- [ ] 438 A SECRET STIRRING, Terri Herrington.......17639-5-38
- [ ] 439 TEARS OF LOVE, Anna Hudson.............18634-X-49
- [ ] 440 AT HIS COMMAND, Helen Conrad...........10351-7-13
- [ ] 441 KNOCKOUT, Joanne Bremer................14563-5-19

At your local bookstore or use this handy coupon for ordering:

Dell DELL READERS SERVICE—DEPT. B1148A
P.O. BOX 1000, PINE BROOK, N.J. 07058

Please send me the above title(s). I am enclosing $_____ (please add 75¢ per copy to cover postage and handling). Send check or money order—no cash or COD's. Please allow 3-4 weeks for shipment. CANADIAN ORDERS: please submit in U.S. dollars.

Ms/Mrs/Mr _____

Address _____

City/State _____ Zip _____

JAYNE CASTLE

excites and delights you with tales of adventure and romance

____TRADING SECRETS

Sabrina had wanted only a casual vacation fling with the rugged Matt. But the extraordinary pull between them made that impossible. So did her growing relationship with his son—and her daring attempt to save the boy's life.
19053-3-15 $3.50

____DOUBLE DEALING

Jayne Castle sweeps you into the corporate world of multimillion dollar real estate schemes and the very private world of executive lovers. Mixing business with pleasure, they made *passion* their bottom line.
12121-3-18 $3.95

At your local bookstore or use this handy coupon for ordering:

Dell DELL READERS SERVICE—DEPT. B1148B
P.O. BOX 1000, PINE BROOK, N.J. 07058

Please send me the above title(s). I am enclosing $_____ (please add 75¢ per copy to cover postage and handling). Send check or money order—no cash or CODs. Please allow 3-4 weeks for shipment.
CANADIAN ORDERS: please submit in U.S. dollars.

Ms./Mrs./Mr._____

Address_____

City/State_____ Zip_____

Rekindle your secret yearnings for romance and passion with the splendid historical novels of

Vanessa Royall

- ___ FIRES OF DELIGHT 12538-3-15 $3.95
- ___ FLAMES OF DESIRE 14637-2-29 2.95
- ___ FIREBRAND'S WOMAN 12597-9-05 2.95
- ___ THE PASSIONATE AND THE PROUD . . 16814-7-11 3.50

At your local bookstore or use this handy coupon for ordering:

Dell DELL READERS SERVICE—DEPT. B1148C
P.O. BOX 1000, PINE BROOK, N.J. 07058

Please send me the above title(s). I am enclosing $_____ (please add 75¢ per copy to cover postage and handling). Send check or money order—no cash or CODs. Please allow 3-4 weeks for shipment. CANADIAN ORDERS: please submit in U.S. dollars.

Ms./Mrs./Mr._____

Address_____

City/State_____ Zip_____